"Mr. Logan?" Lo

Jesse's head snapped
looked as if it had be

Lori hoped she wouldn't live to regret her next words.

"Are you still looking for a nanny?"

"That's right." The words sounded curt. "I didn't realize you were interested in the position. When can you start?" Jesse's words were sarcastic. He must want to scare her off. He'd already fired five nannies in the months since the triplets were born.

Lori met his gaze. And smiled sweetly. She could handle him.

"Right now."

After the Storm:
A Kansas community unites to rebuild

Healing the Boss's Heart—Valerie Hansen
July 2009

Marrying Minister Right—Annie Jones
August 2009

Rekindled Hearts—Brenda Minton
September 2009

The Matchmaking Pact—Carolyne Aarsen
October 2009

A Family for Thanksgiving—Patricia Davids
November 2009

Jingle Bell Babies—Kathryn Springer
December 2009

Books by Kathryn Springer

Love Inspired

Tested by Fire
Her Christmas Wish
By Her Side
For Her Son's Love
Family Treasures
A Treasure Worth Keeping
Hidden Treasures
Jingle Bell Babies

Steeple Hill

Front Porch Princess
Hearts Evergreen
"A Match Made
  for Christmas"
Picket Fence Promises
The Prince Charming List

KATHRYN SPRINGER

is a lifelong Wisconsin resident. Growing up in a "newspaper" family, she spent long hours as a child plunking out stories on her mother's typewriter and hasn't stopped writing since! She loves to write inspirational romance because it allows her to combine her faith in God with her love of a happy ending.

Jingle Bell Babies
Kathryn Springer

Steeple
Hill®

Published by Steeple Hill Books™

Special thanks and acknowledgment to
Kathryn Springer for her contribution to the
After the Storm miniseries.

STEEPLE HILL BOOKS

Steeple
Hill®

Recycling programs
for this product may
not exist in your area.

ISBN-13: 978-0-373-87566-5

JINGLE BELL BABIES

Copyright © 2009 by Harlequin Books S.A.

www.SteepleHill.com

Printed in U.S.A.

Yet this I call to mind and therefore I have hope;
because of the Lord's great love we are not
consumed, for his compassions never fail.
They are new every morning.

—*Lamentations* 3:21–23

To Val, Annie, Brenda, Carolyne and Pat. It was an honor to be able to work with such gifted writers. Your cooperation, encouragement and prayer support over the course of the summer was a real blessing—and I love how we occasionally took "cyber-coffee breaks" together!

Prologue

July 11, 1:15 p.m.

"One of the funnel clouds that touched down in the area yesterday and struck the small town of High Plains was determined to be a level F3. Already the Red Cross, local law enforcement agents and volunteers have banded together to begin cleanup—"

Jesse Logan stabbed his finger against the power button of the radio. He didn't need to hear a reporter condense the past twenty-four hours into a neat sound bite, or try to describe the damage a second funnel cloud had caused when it slashed across the prairie, directly toward the Circle L.

Jesse had seen the devastation firsthand; he was standing in the middle of it.

The kitchen lay in shambles around him. The twister had spared the outbuildings but clipped the side of the ranch house, taking out a section of the wall, while leaving his mother's antique china cabinet in the corner of the room intact. Glass from the shattered window littered the floor, strewn among soggy tufts of insulation and chunks of sodden wallboard.

Jesse picked up a piece of wood and was about to pitch it into the growing pile of debris when he realized it was one of the legs from the kitchen table.

His fingers tightened around it, ignoring the splinters that bit into his skin.

Yesterday morning he'd sat at the table, before going out to do his chores.

And yesterday afternoon…

A fresh wave of pain crashed over Jesse, making him wonder if he wasn't still caught in the throes of a nightmare. Except his eyes weren't closed.

The crunch of tires against gravel momentarily broke through his turbulent thoughts. For a split second hope stirred inside his chest as he sent up a silent prayer that the car coming up the driveway would be a familiar one.

It was.

The hammer slipped out of Jesse's hand and grazed a crease in the hardwood floor as the High Plains squad car stopped in front of the house. Colt Ridgeway's tall frame unfolded from the passenger side.

As the police chief approached, the stoic set of his jaw and the regret darkening his eyes told Jesse everything.

No. No. No.

"This is going to be hard for you to hear, Jesse." His friend's quiet words barely penetrated the rushing sound in Jesse's head. "Late this morning…found Marie's vehicle…tree fell on the driver's side…"

Like a child, Jesse wanted to press his hands against his ears and shut out the truth.

Where are You, God? Are You even listening? How much more do You think one man can take?

The silent cry burst out of a place deep inside him.

Hadn't he gone through enough?

"Marie must have been trying to outrun the tornado," Colt continued softly. "I'm so sorry for your loss, Jesse. Sorry for you…and your girls."

Jesse couldn't answer. Couldn't tell Colt the truth. Not yet. That his wife hadn't been trying to outrun the tornado—she'd been running away. From him.

When the driving rain had forced him to abandon his chores the day before, he found Marie's note on the kitchen table. Next to it, the simple gold wedding band and diamond engagement ring he gave her the night he proposed. An heirloom that had been in the Logan family for generations.

He'd had to read through his wife's letter twice before the meaning sank in but the words had remained branded in his memory.

Jesse,
I have nothing left to give. If I stay on the ranch, I'll never become the person I was meant to be. You were the one who wanted a family, so I'm leaving the babies with you. I'm going back to Kansas City and I'll contact you when I'm settled.
Marie

The storm bending the trees outside hadn't compared to the one raging inside of him.

Frantic, Jesse had immediately called the nurse's station in the Manhattan hospital, where their premature triplets had been in the NICU for the past two months.

The nurse had verified that Marie hadn't shown up that afternoon to sit with the girls.

He braved the weather to drive to the hospital anyway, hoping that his wife had had a change of heart and gone there instead of the airport.

She hadn't.

Jesse stayed with his daughters the rest of the evening, waiting for a phone call. It wasn't until one of the nurses on duty had asked him if his ranch was located near High Plains that he learned about the tornadoes.

Unable to get through to his hired hands or his sister, Maya, Jesse spent a sleepless night in the family lounge and most of the morning waiting for the state police to remove the barricades from the roads.

When he was finally able to return to the ranch, Jesse had gone from room to room, calling Marie's name. Praying that news of the storm would have fanned an ember of concern in her heart and brought her home. If not for him, then for Madison, Brooke and Sasha.

At the thought of his precious girls, Jesse was struck by an overwhelming desire to hold them again.

"I have to get back to the hospital." He pushed past Colt.

"Jesse, wait. Don't be stubborn." Colt put a restraining hand on his arm. "You're in no shape to go anywhere. Let me call someone for you."

He immediately thought of his younger brother, Clay, but he shook the image away. Colt was right. He wasn't thinking clearly.

His sister, Maya, should have been the one who came to mind first. Not Clay. Clay had shirked his responsibility to the ranch and the family years ago.

If his brother hadn't even bothered to call when Maya had told him Jesse's triplets were struggling for their lives in the NICU, what made him think Clay would be here for him now?

In that respect, Marie and Clay had been alike. Both of them ran away when things got hard. Jesse knew it was up to him to pick up the pieces. Alone. Again.

He swallowed hard against the lump lodged in his throat. "I'll call Maya," he managed to rasp.

"Jesse…" Colt frowned.

Don't say it, Jesse thought. His self-control was hanging by a thread. He couldn't think about his own grief though, he had to think about the three babies he'd left sleeping peacefully in their cribs only a few hours ago. He had to keep it together. For his daughters.

As if Colt could read his mind, he nodded slowly. "I understand. And don't worry about the…arrangements right now, Jess. Take as much time as you need."

The automatic doors parted as Jesse reached the front of the building. He'd spent so much time at the hospital over the past eight weeks that many of the staff knew him by name. Two volunteer auxiliary workers stopped talking and nodded solemnly when he passed the information desk.

He'd only taken a few steps down the corridor when a man stepped out of the cafeteria and intercepted him.

"Jesse."

Jesse froze at the sound of the familiar voice, although he barely recognized his father-in-law. The deep lines in Philip Banner's face and the haunted look in his eyes told Jesse he already knew about Marie's death.

Instinctively, Jesse extended his hand to grasp his father-in-law's, but the man stepped away, rebuffing the overture.

Jesse flinched. Philip had never bothered to hide his disapproval. As one of the state's leading prosecutors, Marie's father had had high hopes his only child would marry well. A cattle rancher from Kansas didn't fit his model of the ideal son-in-law. Philip and Sharon had kept in close touch with their daughter after the wedding, but barely acknowledged Jesse's existence.

Jesse had hoped his in-laws would soften when they found out they were going to be grandparents, but if anything, the news had made them more resentful. Instead of anticipating the girls' arrival, Sharon seemed to blame Jesse for Marie's difficult pregnancy.

"Have you seen the girls yet?" It occurred to Jesse that Philip and Sharon may have come to the hospital for the same reason he had. To hold the triplets and try to find some comfort in knowing that a part of Marie lived on in her daughters.

Philip ignored the question. "Sharon and I need your permission to take Marie…" His voice cracked and he looked away, as if it were difficult to look Jesse in the eye.

Jesse stared at the man, unable to comprehend what he was asking. And then the truth hit him. They hadn't shown up out of concern for Jesse. Or his baby girls. His in-laws had been close by because they'd been part of Marie's exit plan. They'd probably made arrangements to meet her at the airport—to lend their support in case Jesse followed—before escorting her back to Kansas City.

"You want to take her—" Jesse couldn't say the word *body* "—back to Kansas City?"

"We have a family plot in the cemetery." Philip's expression changed and now bitterness scored the words. "Marie never belonged here with you. You know that. Last week she called and asked us if she could come home. It's where she wanted to be. It's where she should be now."

Home.

Jesse had a flashback of the day the obstetrician told them the ultrasound revealed they were expecting triplets.

Jesse's initial shock had quickly changed to delight. He'd always wanted a large family. When it came right down to it, what difference did it make whether there were years or minutes between the births of their children?

And if he were honest with himself, he'd hoped that starting a family would ease the tension growing between them.

During their courtship, Marie claimed she couldn't wait to have children, but after the wedding she'd avoided the topic. Jesse hadn't minded it being just the two of them for a while, but Marie's reaction when she'd found out she was pregnant had disturbed him. Overwhelmed, she'd started to cry and begged him to take her home.

He'd thought she meant the ranch.

Now, seeing the anger and grief on his father-in-law's face, Jesse was forced to admit the truth behind Philip's claim: Marie had never considered the ranch her home.

Jesse had lost his wife long before the tornado struck.

The words stuck in his throat but he pushed them out. "I'll talk to the director at the funeral home. The two of you can work out the arrangements."

Philip nodded curtly, pivoted and walked away without

a backward glance. No *thank-you*. No mention of his granddaughters.

The little energy Jesse had left drained away. On emotional autopilot, he took the elevator to the NICU. When he reached the nursery, he heard someone singing softly to the girls.

But it wasn't his sister.

Sitting beside the crib where his daughters slept was Lori Martin, the young, auburn-haired nurse he'd met once or twice. Jesse hadn't gotten to know her as well as he had the other nurses, because her shift ended before he arrived to sit with the girls every evening.

The soft smile on Lori's face and the expression in her eyes made Jesse's chest tighten.

It wasn't right.

Marie should have been the one singing to them. Loving them. And yet she'd left them...all of them.

Jesse's fists clenched at his sides.

Marie was gone, but he had three reasons to live: his daughters. And Jesse decided to make sure no one would hurt them again.

Chapter One

December

"You could have given Maya some hope."

Jesse stiffened at the sound of Clay's quiet voice behind him.

The memory of their sister's stricken expression had seared Jesse's conscience. He knew he'd been out of line, but the last thing he needed was his younger brother beating him up about it.

He'd been doing a pretty good job of that all by himself.

"Maya's been worried sick since Tommy ran away," Clay pointed out. "All she needed was to hear you say you'd find her son and bring him home."

"I did say that."

"'I'll bring him home *either way,* Maya.'" Clay's voice deepened—an exaggerated imitation of Jesse's low baritone—as he recited the words Jesse had spoken just before leaving the house. "In my opinion, you could have left two little words out of that promise."

"I don't remember asking for your opinion." Jesse tightened the cinch on Saber's saddle before leading the gelding from the stall. "Is it fair to give Maya false hope?"

"Now, are you asking my opinion?"

Jesse scowled. Since Clay's unexpected return to High Plains a month ago, his brother claimed to have changed. Jesse didn't believe it for a second. Not when Clay still managed to get to him like a burr under a saddle blanket.

"Maya needed encouragement. Would it have been so hard to give her some instead of being...Mr. Gloom and Doom?"

Jesse felt the sting of the insult. "*You're* telling me what Maya needs?"

"I know I messed up by leaving." Clay met his gaze. "But that's all in the past now."

"How convenient."

Clay's jaw tightened, the only outward sign that Jesse's words had found their mark. "If I remember correctly, you were always the glass half-full guy in the family."

That was before his glass got tipped over—and stepped on.

"I can't tell Maya that Tommy's all right if I don't know it's true." Jesse wanted to believe they'd find Tommy safe and sound. The whole family—Jesse included—had embraced the precocious little boy. Even before Maya had married Gregory Garrison, and they'd started formal adoption proceedings, Tommy had become part of the family. As far as Jesse was concerned, signing the adoption papers was merely a formality. He'd been "Uncle Jesse" for months.

But he had to deal with facts, whether anyone else wanted to or not. And the facts—that Tommy was only six years old and had been missing for three days—didn't exactly tip the balance in their favor.

When they'd discovered Tommy had run away, volunteer search parties formed immediately, to comb the area. Colt Ridgeway even arranged for a search-and-rescue dog to aid in the effort. But the ranch's vast acreage—ordinarily a source of pride for Jesse—had worked against them.

After Tommy disappeared, Maya had taken a quick inventory and found that he'd taken some food, his coat and a backpack. The discovery had eased their minds—for the first twenty-four hours. But as resourceful as the little guy had proven to be, a coat wasn't enough to ward off the December wind penetrating the sheepskin lining of Jesse's jacket. And food eventually ran out....

Jesse decided to change the subject before he said something else he might regret. "Be sure to tell Nicki that I appreciate her willingness to watch the triplets again today, while I look for Tommy."

"She knows." There was a glint in Clay's eyes. "And don't you mean while *we* look for Tommy?"

Jesse stepped out of the barn and stopped short at the sight of Sundance, an ornery pinto mare, saddled up and ready to go. Her pinned ears let him know she wasn't very happy about the situation.

He hesitated, tempted to change his plan in order to watch Sundance send his brother into orbit. Maybe another time. "You remember the lay of the land. It would make sense for you to take another group out."

"It might," Clay agreed. "But I'm going with you."

"I'll make better time by myself."

A shadow crossed Clay's face, but then he shrugged. "Even the Lone Ranger had Tonto."

"And Edgar Bergen had Charlie McCarthy," Jesse muttered.

"Do I need to remind you that I'm a grown man and 'you're not the boss of me' anymore?"

Hearing the familiar quip made Jesse's lips twitch. Clay had hurled those words at him frequently while growing up. There was a reason he'd wanted to break away from the rest of the search parties and go it alone. But for some reason, Jesse found himself giving in.

The gleam of laughter in his brother's eyes brought back memories of a time when they'd actually been at ease in each other's company. Before Clay dove into teenage rebellion and turned his back on everything Jesse believed in.

They'd come to an uneasy truce at Thanksgiving, when Clay asked if he could move back to the ranch. Jesse guessed the request had something to do with the lovesick look in his brother's eye whenever his new fiancée, Nicki Appleton, came into view, but some things were hard to let go of. Clay had walked away from his birthright once before. What was to say he wouldn't do it again?

As they passed the house, Jesse saw Maya step out onto the wide front porch. Regret sawed against his conscience again. Not because he'd spoken the truth but because it had hurt his sister.

"Give her some hope," Clay had said.

How could Jesse explain that he and hope had parted company six months ago? If the road to hope led to disappointment, what was the point?

By the time they reached the gate, Maya was waiting for them.

Jesse had to force himself to look his sister in the eye.

When he did, the light he saw shining there was a far cry from the worry that had darkened those eyes earlier.

"Michael just called." Maya no longer referred to the minister of High Plains Community Church—her new husband's cousin—by his formal title. "He and Heather Waters are organizing a candlelight prayer vigil for Tommy this evening. He said the people who can't physically join in the search felt led to join together and pray. I know you and Clay are going to find him today, Jesse. I can *feel* it. God is going to show you the way."

Jesse tried to hide his frustration. Maya's faith had always been her North Star, pointing toward the truth. Not too long ago, his sister's unwavering conviction would have challenged him. Strengthened him. But now the only thing her words stirred inside of Jesse were the ashes of what remained of his dreams.

"Keep believing, Maya." Clay came up alongside her. He leaned over the saddle and pulled her into his arms, ruffling her hair as if she were Tommy's age. "God knows exactly where Tommy is. And you're right. We're going to find him. By nine o'clock tonight you'll be tucking him into bed."

Jesse wanted to put a muzzle on his brother. How could Clay get Maya's hopes up like that? Was he the only person in Kansas who was willing to face things the way they were, instead of the way he wanted them to be?

Maya aimed a grateful look at Clay and her smile came out in full force. For the first time in three days.

Jesse clicked his tongue and Saber agreeably stepped forward. The minute they passed through the gate, he nudged the gelding into a canter.

Unfortunately, Clay caught up to him before Jesse's temper had time to cool. "Was that really necessary?"

Clay didn't pretend to misunderstand him. "Yes."

"You shouldn't let her hope for the best."

"And you shouldn't let her imagine the worst," Clay retorted.

Hadn't they already had this conversation?

Jesse wondered if they'd ever see eye to eye on anything.

He tamped down his anger, bit his tongue and forced himself to focus on the reason he'd teamed up with Clay in the first place.

Tommy.

After the boy disappeared, the county sheriff had organized the search, dividing up Jesse's property on a map and assigning each group of volunteers a certain section. Given Tommy's age and size, they'd started close to the ranch house and gradually expanded the search to include the hills and grazing land.

The teams had met back at the ranch after a fruitless search earlier that morning, and when the sheriff instructed everyone to recheck the areas they'd already searched, a shiver of unease had skated through Jesse.

Staring down at the map, he had had an overwhelming urge to scrap the grid and go with his gut. And his gut told him not to waste time covering the same ground again.

He just hadn't expected his brother to tag along.

They rode in silence until Jesse turned his horse down a worn cow path.

"Where are we going?"

"The river," Jesse replied curtly.

To his surprise, his prodigal brother followed without a peep. Accustomed to Clay chafing every time Jesse took the lead, he found he couldn't let that slide. "No argument? No 'do you really think a kid Tommy's age could have made it that far on his own'?"

"You did."

Jesse twisted around in the saddle to stare at his brother.

"It's a long shot," Clay continued. "I mean, you went to the cave on horseback and Tommy is on foot."

Jesse's mouth dropped open. "Cave?"

"Oh, don't look so surprised. It wasn't much of a secret. I followed you there all the time."

"You followed me." Jesse couldn't believe it. He'd been certain the secret hiding place he'd discovered had actually *been* a secret.

The ranch had been his playground as a child, and he'd explored every inch of it. And not always with his parents' permission or his siblings' knowledge, either. At least, he *thought* it had been without his siblings' knowledge.

"Of course I did." Clay's shoulder lifted in a casual shrug. "But I knew you wanted to be alone, so I let you think you were."

Wanted to be alone...

Bits and pieces of a conversation he'd had with Tommy suddenly trickled through Jesse's memory like the beginning of a rock slide. And then it all came crashing back.

Thanksgiving Day, Tommy had complained that Layla, Maya's three-year-old daughter, was always following him. In the name of male bonding, Jesse had sympathized and told Tommy that his irritation was perfectly normal. He confided that as a boy he also had times when he needed to get away from his younger sister and brother.

"Did you go to your room and lock the door?" Tommy had asked.

Jesse had laughed at the question. He and Clay had always shared a bedroom, so there'd been no privacy there.

That's when he mentioned his favorite "thinking spot" had been a secret cave, its location marked by a strange U-shaped tree whose roots formed the ceiling of the hideaway.

Jesse's mouth suddenly felt as dry as dust. What he'd failed to mention to Tommy was that the last time he'd checked the cave—about five years ago—it had collapsed.

"Jesse? What's wrong?"

Instead of answering, Jesse urged Saber down the hill.

"I really appreciate you helping out at the last minute, Lori."

"I'm glad you called." Lori Martin flashed a quick smile in Nicki Appleton's direction as she peeled off her coat and hung it on a colorful, rainbow-shaped wall peg. "I worked today and missed the e-mail about the prayer vigil."

"Reverend Garrison pulled it together pretty quickly, but when I offered to oversee the nursery tonight, I had no idea there'd be such a large turnout." Nicki smiled and blew a wisp of curly blond hair out of her eyes. "I definitely have my hands full in here. I'll give you a choice, though, since you came to my rescue tonight. Do you want to give the triplets their bottles or play demolition derby with the boys over there in the corner?"

The triplets.

Instinctively Lori moved toward the three infant seats arranged in a semicircle on the floor where Nicki sat. Sure enough, there were the Logan girls, a trio of adorable little blossoms dressed in various shades of pink.

She hadn't seen them since October, when she'd volunteered to take a turn in the nursery during the morning worship service. She'd been thrilled at how much the girls had changed—but a little taken aback that the strong connection she'd felt for them hadn't.

As a nurse who provided specialized care for premature infants, Lori walked a fine line between providing the best care possible while not letting herself get too emotionally attached. But from the moment she'd witnessed those tiny girls in the incubator, she'd fallen in love.

Maybe it was because Marie Logan, the babies' mother, had spent more time sipping coffee and flipping through magazines in the family lounge than she had sitting next to her daughters' cribs.

Lori tried to be understanding. It was never easy for a new mother to be released from the hospital and have to leave her children behind. But right from the beginning, Marie seemed to be consumed with her own needs rather than the needs of her daughters. She treated the nursing staff as if they were her personal servants, and her constant criticism frequently brought the aides to tears.

At the end of one particularly stressful morning, Lori took Marie aside and asked if she could pray with her. Marie's bitter response chilled her.

"The reason I'm here is because God is punishing me for my mistakes. It's not like He's going to listen to anything I have to say."

Before Lori had a chance to convince Marie that wasn't true, the woman had fled from the room. Several days later, Marie's body was recovered in the wreckage from the tornado.

Rumors flew around the pediatric ward that Marie had left her husband and the babies shortly before the tornado struck High Plains. Lori didn't want to believe it, but the day Jesse Logan had arrived to take the triplets home, she'd seen the truth etched in the deep lines fanning out from his eyes.

Midnight-blue eyes that were a perfect match to the ones staring solemnly up at her.

"I'll feed the triplets." Lori reached for Sasha and was rewarded with a beautiful heart-melting baby grin.

Only three and a half pounds at birth, Sasha had been the smallest of the trio. She'd also fought the hardest to survive.

By the time Sasha left the hospital—a full week after her two sisters—she'd stolen the hearts of the entire nursing staff.

"Are you sure?" Nicki raised a teasing brow. "They remind me of a nest of baby birds who all want their dinner at the same time."

"I help, too." A bright-eyed, pajama-clad toddler drifted over and hugged Nicki's arm.

"That's the truth." Nicki gave her foster daughter an affectionate squeeze. "Kasey has been a big help with the babies over the past few days."

Lori grinned as Sasha latched on to the bottle with both hands, as if she hadn't eaten for days. "When did you start taking care of the Logans?"

"It's not permanent. I've been helping out with the girls while Clay and Jesse look for Tommy Jacobs." Nicki's expression clouded. "That's why they organized the prayer vigil tonight. He's been missing for three days and…it's taking a toll on the family."

Lori imagined that was an understatement. She'd heard about Tommy through the prayer chain at High Plains Community and wasn't surprised to learn that Maya's older brothers had taken an active role in looking for their nephew. Or that the entire congregation had reached out to the family.

"I don't mind helping Jesse out when he needs a sitter now and then, but between Kasey and my job at the preschool, I have my hands full," Nicki continued. "I'm not sure who is going to take over and be Nanny Number Six."

Lori's attention, which had been irresistibly drawn to Sasha's tiny fingers, snapped back to Nicki.

Number six?

"Are you saying that Jesse Logan has gone through five nannies?"

"In five months." Nicki nodded. "That has to be some kind of record."

Lori silently agreed. And she couldn't believe the five nannies had all been at fault. Anyone taking on the enormous responsibility of caring for triplets—and premature ones at that—would accept the job with a clear understanding of the challenges they would face.

What had happened?

A sudden image of the handsome but stern-faced rancher flashed in Lori's mind. She couldn't imagine Jesse being an easy man to work for.

"The last nanny Jesse fired had only been at the ranch for forty-eight hours," Nicki continued. "She put in an application at the preschool where I teach, but was embarrassed to tell the director why Jesse had let her go. Apparently, he had a problem with the bedtime songs she sang to the triplets."

"You're kidding."

"I wish I were." Nicki sighed. "Anyway, the word is out, and no one has responded to the classified ad Jesse put in the newspaper for the last two weeks. Clay and I are praying that the right woman comes along. Soon."

A memory stirred in Lori's mind but she immediately pushed it aside. It bounced back.

Not a good sign.

The day after the tornado, she'd been called in early to cover another nurse's shift. Everyone was shaken by the news of the devastation, and with tears in her eyes, one of the nurses whispered to Lori that she'd heard Marie Logan had died.

Lori knew the triplets had no comprehension that their lives had been irrevocably changed, but she'd gone to them immediately. And while she sat next to the crib and sang to the girls, she'd felt someone's presence in the room.

Jesse stood in the doorway, watching her.

She'd wanted to comfort him—to tell him she was praying for him—but the hard look in his eyes warned her that he wouldn't welcome any sympathy.

As Lori slipped out of the room, she'd asked God to let her know if there was a way she could help the Logan family.

Had He waited five months to give her an answer?

Chapter Two

Discouragement gnawed at Jesse as he paused to survey the barren landscape. The frontline winds that had spawned the funnel cloud in July had left their mark on this end of the property, too.

"Jess—wait a second."

Jesse glanced back and saw Clay dismount and reach for something in the brush.

Jesse's heart kicked against his chest. Ever since the tornado, he'd been searching for the heirloom engagement ring Marie had left on the kitchen table that day. He'd found the soggy remains of the note and her wedding band in the rubble, but there'd been no sign of the diamond.

Several times a week for the past five months, Maya faithfully checked the community Lost and Found to see if anyone had turned it in. Reverend Garrison had even made a special announcement during one of the community meetings to let everyone know how much the ring meant to the Logan family. One weekend, he'd even brought his teenage niece, Avery, and a small volunteer crew from the youth group out to the ranch to comb a section of the property for missing items.

"I can't believe how far a twister can carry little things like this," Clay remarked, examining something in his palm.

"What is it?" If Clay had found the ring, he'd have told Jesse right away. Silently, Jesse berated himself for giving hope a temporary foothold.

Hadn't he learned that particular lesson already?

"A key chain…with a whistle on it."

Jesse was at his brother's side in two strides. "Let me see that."

Clay's eyebrow shot up. "It's yours?"

Jesse stared at the piece of plastic cradled in his brother's palm. "It's Tommy's."

"The tornado dropped it this far from town?"

The tornado. Or Tommy.

On a hunch, Jesse raised the whistle to his lips and blew.

Clay winced. "Making sure it still works?"

"Shh." For a moment, Jesse thought he'd imagined the faint cry woven into the wind. But Clay's sharp inhale told Jesse he'd heard it, too.

"Uncle J-Jesse?" The roots of an overturned tree moved and a familiar freckled face poked out.

When Tommy saw the two men standing there, he scrambled out of his hiding spot and barreled toward them.

Jesse swung the boy up into his arms and Tommy burst into tears.

As Clay radioed the good news to the deputy in charge of the search, Jesse settled Tommy in the saddle in front of him and buttoned him into his coat. The boy's ragged sigh shook his thin frame and went straight through Jesse.

He still couldn't believe that Tommy had managed to stumble upon the collapsed cave.

When the tornado had chewed its way across the property, it upended the tree that had once marked the cave's location, but created an opening large enough for a six-year-old boy to squeeze into. Sheltering him not only from the elements but from any predators lurking in the area.

Clay had murmured something about answered prayer. Jesse hadn't argued the point. Maybe God had stopped listening to him, but at least He had heard Maya. At the moment, Jesse could be grateful for that.

"Are you sure Mom…Maya…and G-Greg aren't mad at me?" The words were muffled but Jesse could hear the undercurrent of worry in Tommy's voice.

Jesse frowned. Tommy had been calling Maya and his brother-in-law "Mom and Dad" for the past few months.

"I'm sure. They've been worried about you…." His throat tightened. They'd *all* been worried about him. "And they're going to be happy to know that you're okay."

"Even if I did sumpthin' bad?"

"What do you mean?"

"I made Layla cry. Not on purpose," Tommy added quickly. "But I don't think they believed me. And then I heard Maya tell you there's a problem with the 'doption. I know what that means. There's a problem with *me*."

Jesse sucked in a breath. No one could figure out why Tommy had run away from home, but now it all made sense. He'd overheard part of a conversation Jesse had had with Maya.

"Believe me, Tommy, that's not what she meant. Everyone loves you—you're part of the family."

"For real?" Tommy's chin tilted toward Jesse and the dirt-smudged face brightened.

"For real. The problem with the adoption isn't you, champ. The problem is that it isn't going as fast as Maya and Greg would like it to," Jesse explained. "Trust me. They can't *wait* for you to be their little boy."

Tommy snuggled against him. "We better get back so she isn't worried anymore. I'm glad you came, Uncle Jesse. I was getting kinda cold. And I ran out of—" he battled a yawn "—peanut butter."

"They found him." Nicki picked up Kasey and twirled her around in the middle of the room, much to the toddler's delight. "Clay just called my cell phone. Tommy is fine. Tired and hungry, but fine. Maya and Greg are meeting Jesse at home."

Lori closed her eyes and offered a silent prayer of thanks.

"I'm going to sneak into the service and tell Reverend Garrison so he can announce the good news." Nicki spun one more wobbly pirouette as she glided toward the doorway with Kasey in her arms. "Thanks for staying to help, Lori. I'm sure you had other plans for the evening. Plans that *didn't* include total chaos!"

Lori smiled but didn't confess that total chaos was a welcome change from her silent apartment, a bowl of pretzels and the latest cozy mystery she'd picked up at the grocery store checkout.

While Nicki entertained Kasey and the other children throughout the evening, Lori devoted her attention to the triplets.

Brooke and Madison had taken their bottles and had eventually fallen asleep, but Sasha was clearly a night owl. The baby remained wide-awake, content to cuddle in Lori's lap as they put several miles on the rocking chair.

Lori, who held and cared for babies all day, couldn't ignore the deep connection she felt with the triplets. Several times during the course of the evening, Nicki had commented on how comfortable they seemed to be with her.

It seemed unlikely they would remember her....

Lori glanced down and met Sasha's solemn gaze.

If she didn't know better, she'd think that Sasha was reminding her of the promise she made to God that day.

It wasn't exactly a promise. More like an...offer.

A suggestion, really.

"I love my job at the hospital," Lori murmured out loud. "They need me."

Sasha, who'd been cheerful most of the evening, suddenly let loose a heart-wrenching whimper.

The timing of which had to be an absolute coincidence, Lori decided.

"Oh, no, you don't. That's not fair." She lifted Sasha higher in her arms, nuzzling the rose-kissed cheek. Encouraged by the baby's soft chortle of laughter, Lori closed her eyes and planted a trail of noisy kisses up the baby's pudgy arm.

Sasha's tiny feet began to pedal rapidly inside the flannel blanket.

"Oh, really? I can find little toes, too, so you better—"

A door to the nursery snapped shut and Lori's eyes flew open.

And there stood Jesse Logan.

His sharp, blue-eyed gaze flickered over the infant

seats near Lori's feet where Brooke and Madison slept, before moving to Sasha, who recognized her daddy and gurgled happily, waving her arms to get his attention.

Lori gave Sasha points for bravery.

How—for even a split second—could she have entertained the notion that God wanted *her* to be Nanny Number Six?

Jesse didn't look like a man who needed anyone's help.

Although there was no getting around the fact that the man was extremely handsome, the set of his jaw didn't look as though it allowed much movement—and certainly not on something as frivolous as a smile. The silky fringe of dark hair beneath his Stetson didn't soften features that looked as if they'd been sculpted by the elements.

"Mr. Logan." Lori rose to her feet, gently trying to disengage her shirt from Sasha's grip.

There was a spark of recognition in his eyes.

A thought suddenly occurred to Lori, and she lifted her free hand to her hair for a quick, exploratory search. At one point during the evening, Kasey had clipped a pink elephant barrette on the end of Lori's braid.

Yup. Still there.

Lori suddenly wished she hadn't run home to exchange her scrubs for faded jeans and a sweatshirt. At the hospital, there'd been a professional boundary in place. Jesse Logan—patients' father; Lori Martin—nurse.

But now? Now she was simply a Good Samaritan. A Good Samaritan whose hair was in a tangle from being tugged on by—count them—*six* little hands all evening. And then Kasey had added her own special touch.

"Where is Nicki?" Jesse's loose-limbed stride carried him across the room in less than two seconds.

Now he stood close enough for Lori to pick up the subtle, earthy scent of wind and leather that clung to his coat.

Lori wasn't petite by any standards, but she had to tip her chin up to look at him. His height was a little intimidating. And so was his expression.

Instinctively, she tightened her hold on Sasha.

"Nicki is talking to Reverend Garrison. My name is on the sub list for the church nursery, so she asked if I was free to help her watch the children this evening." Lori wasn't a babbler by nature, but there was something unnerving about being with a man who didn't waste words. Not to mention a man who didn't seem to like to *use* them, either. "I don't know if you remember, but we met—"

"I remember you."

Okay, then.

Lori tried again. "The girls have really grown." She couldn't prevent a chuckle. "But they haven't changed all that much, have they?"

Jesse's finger flicked the brim of his cowboy hat, pushing it up. The movement chased the shadows away, revealing the full impact of cobalt-blue eyes set in a face stained a deep golden brown from the sun.

"What do you mean?" Those eyes narrowed and Lori realized he'd taken her comment as a criticism. "Their pediatrician says they're developing on schedule."

"I meant their personalities," Lori explained, wondering if she'd just witnessed the same look the five nannies had seen moments before they'd been fired.

No wonder he was having a difficult time filling the position!

"Brooke still lets you know that she wants something *yesterday*." She smiled down at the baby, who continued to move restlessly even in sleep. "And you know Madison is going to be the peacemaker of the group. When Brooke started crying tonight, Madison offered her own thumb to calm her down. And Sasha's quiet, but she takes in everything around her—"

"You can tell them apart?"

Lori blinked at the terse interruption. "Can't you?"

"Of course I can." Clearly offended, Jesse swept off his hat and tunneled his hand through his hair. "Maddie is bald, Brooke has a birthmark on her left shoulder blade and Sasha is the smallest."

Lori stared at him in amazement. He'd zeroed in on some of the triplets' physical characteristics.

Didn't the man realize his daughters had three very distinct *personalities? Temperaments?*

Needs?

It suddenly became important for Lori to make Jesse understand.

"It's not just what they *look* like on the outside. Madison loves to be cuddled but Brooke doesn't have the patience for it. My guess is that she'll be the first one to crawl. Sasha is attracted to color and motion…."

Lori's voice broke off as Jesse dropped to one knee in front of Madison's infant seat.

Conversation over.

She'd lost him. It suddenly occurred to Lori that Jesse Logan was probably the type of man whose entire life revolved around his ranch. A man who believed that providing food and a roof over their heads made him a good father to his daughters.

The second-shift nurses had all raved about Jesse's devotion to his children because he'd shown up at the

NICU every night. That didn't prove anything to Lori. Sitting beside their cribs could have simply been one more thing for Jesse Logan to check off his to-do list. A duty instead of an act of love.

They'll need more, Lori wanted to protest. *So much more.*

Jesse's indifference raked over debris from her past and scraped up old memories. Memories that Lori thought had long been put to rest.

"What do you want from me, Roxanne? I said I'd own up to my responsibility and I did...but that doesn't mean I have to pretend to be happy about it...."

Lori swallowed hard and tried to shut out her father's voice, shaken that the words sounded as clear as if he'd spoken them the day before, instead of fifteen years ago.

The room began to shrink and Lori felt an overwhelming urge to escape.

"I'll find Nicki." With Sasha still in her arms, Lori headed toward the door.

She wasn't surprised when Jesse didn't respond.

Emotions churned inside of her. How could she leave the triplets, when they needed someone who would lavish attention and love on them?

When they needed *her.*

She made her decision. Pausing in the doorway, she turned and looked over her shoulder...

Just in time to see Jesse cup his hands over his mouth and blow on his fingers. Warming them.

Lori's breath caught in her throat.

And that's when she saw it. The subtle sway of his body before he managed to balance his weight on the heels of his boots. The slight dip of his shoulders beneath the heavy coat.

Exhaustion.

The bone-deep kind that sucked away a person's energy—chiseled holes in their perspective. The kind that stole a person's ability to think.

And talk.

Lori's feet felt rooted to the floor and her heart began to pound. "Mr. Logan?"

Jesse's head snapped up and once again his face looked as if it had been carved out of stone.

Lori hoped she wouldn't live to regret her next words. "Are you still looking for a nanny?"

Jesse tried not to let his frustration show.

Of course Lori Martin had heard he was looking for a new nanny. The entire population of High Plains probably knew he was looking for a new nanny.

He'd fired two or three—okay, so maybe it had been five—although he wasn't sure if he could count the last one. Just when he'd opened his mouth to say the words *you're fired,* she'd beaten him to the punch and informed him that she quit. But did that mean he deserved to be treated like a pariah? The last time he'd gone to the newspaper to put in an ad for another caregiver, the woman behind the reception desk had actually laughed. *Laughed.*

Was it his fault that none of the nannies he'd hired had been able to do the job properly?

His sweet-tempered sister's popularity had opened the door to a few favors. But so far, nothing permanent.

He'd been grateful to Nicki for agreeing to watch the triplets over the past few days while they searched for Tommy, but she had her hands full with Kasey, the active toddler she'd recently been granted permission to adopt.

Clay had offered to shoulder more responsibility in the

mornings so Jesse could drive the girls to a day care in High Plains, but that was his last resort. And he had to make that decision in about six hours.

Pride stopped him from letting anyone see how desperate he was. Especially the young, brown-eyed nurse who'd managed to coax a belly laugh out of somber little Sasha.

He could still hear the lilt of Lori's laughter, mingled with his daughter's, as he'd stood outside the door of the church nursery. It had rolled over him with the warmth of a spring breeze. And the sight of her raining kisses on Sasha's chubby arm affected Jesse more than he cared to admit.

"That's right." The words sounded curt, even to his own ears, but it was the best he could do.

Small talk was simply beyond his capability at the moment.

Three days of searching for Tommy, in addition to keeping up with his regular chores and getting up with the triplets during the night, had begun to take its toll. His limbs felt as if they'd been replaced with wet concrete.

Lori Martin lingered in the doorway and Jesse wished she'd go away. And not because his gaze strayed to the soft tendrils of sunset-red hair that had escaped from her braid. Or because Sasha looked perfectly content to remain in the woman's arms.

Nope. Because he was practically dead on his feet and didn't need any witnesses to the fact. Someone who would report back to Nicki. Who'd report to Clay. Who'd report to Maya....

He had an idea. As much as Lori Martin obviously loved children, he knew exactly what would make her beat a hasty retreat.

"I didn't realize you were interested in the position.

When can you start?" Jesse injected just enough sarcasm to scare her off. And let her know exactly what he thought about people gossiping about him.

Lori Martin met his gaze. And smiled sweetly.

"Right now."

Chapter Three

You're hired.

Those two simple words echoed in Lori's mind as she reached the end of the long dirt road, and the car's headlights illuminated a turn-of-the-century two-story house with a stone foundation.

Jesse's house.

Maybe she should leave the engine running.

Lori hadn't expected Jesse to turn cartwheels at her impulsive offer the night before, but his cool response had her questioning her decision. And her sanity.

I can do all things through Him who strengthens me.

The verse in Philippians she'd read during her devotional time that morning filtered through her panic and calmed what some people would have called "the butterflies" in her stomach. To Lori, it felt more like a herd of mustangs had taken up residence there.

She took a deep breath and turned off the ignition.

The front door opened and Jesse stepped onto the porch, his lean, broad-shouldered frame backlit by the soft glow from the window.

He'd been waiting for her.

Lori got out of the car, tempted to leave her suitcase in the trunk. Just in case.

I can do all things through Christ, Lori reminded herself. *All things.*

She'd made a promise to the girls—and to God—and she intended to keep it.

Scraping up her courage, Lori popped the trunk and wrestled her suitcase out. She took a step back and smacked into something warm and solid.

"I can take this." Jesse's fingers closed over the handle and brushed against hers as he took control of the suitcase.

The chilly morning air was making her shiver. Had to be that....

"Thank you." The mustangs had multiplied, but Lori forced a smile.

"Is this all you have?" She sensed a scowl in the darkness.

"I packed what I needed to get me through the next few days." If she lasted that long. "My rental came furnished, but I plan to pick up the rest my things later in the week."

Jesse acknowledged her words with a curt nod as he retraced his steps back to the house.

Did the man know how to smile?

All things...

The verse dissolved like sugar in water as Lori followed Jesse inside and caught her first glimpse of her new home.

"You can go on in." Jesse's gruff prompt encouraged her to take another step forward.

A *reluctant* step forward.

It was obvious that two bachelor ranchers and three babies equaled chaos.

Jesse coughed as he ushered her into the living room. "The place is a little…neglected. I had a housekeeper. Up until last week."

So. He'd fired her, too.

Which explained why the room looked as if the tornado had gone through his house the day before, instead of five months ago.

Bright plastic toys were scattered like confetti from one end of the room to the other. Laundry—men's faded chambray work shirts mixed in with tiny, colorful sleepers—lay draped over the three infant swings lined up in front of the window.

And what was that smell?

Lori took a few more steps forward and something crunched beneath her foot. Glancing down, she saw the remains of a pretzel ground into the carpet.

"The housekeeper did most of the cooking, too." Jesse discreetly swiped up a sock and crossed his arms to hide it from view.

Not that they'd had much time to talk about her specific duties yet, but it would have been nice if Jesse had mentioned she would be in charge, not only of the triplets, but of the entire household.

"I started asking around to find someone else, but…" His voice trailed off and Lori filled in the blanks.

Your former nannies spread the word about you.

The former nannies he'd apparently fired without a qualm.

But Madison, Brooke and Sasha needed her, so Lori was determined not to start off the day—let alone the first fifteen minutes—on the wrong foot.

"Don't worry about it. I don't mind cooking," she said

cheerfully. "I make the best eggplant Parmesan you've ever tasted."

"Eggplant…" Jesse frowned. "I don't think I've ever tried that."

"Oh, I'm sure you'd remember if you had. It's delicious. In fact, it's considered a staple in a vegetarian diet." But probably missing from the menu of a certain cattle rancher.

"Vege—" Jesse choked on the rest of the word. "You're a…vegetarian?"

Lori waited a beat, hoping he'd realize he was being teased. It would prove a sense of humor lurked somewhere below that serious demeanor. "No."

Jesse frowned.

Apparently not. "I was kidding."

"Kidding?" Jesse repeated the word suspiciously.

"Making a joke…." *Never mind.*

"Right." Jesse continued to stare at her, and Lori wondered if, in spite of her best intentions, she was going to break her predecessor's forty-eight-hour record. Abruptly, Jesse turned away. "I'll show you to your room. The girls are still asleep, but I guess that's not a surprise, considering how late they went to bed last night."

Lori envied them. She'd stared at the ceiling for hours, asking God if she'd made the right decision.

It wasn't as if she were a risk-taker by nature. And considering Jesse Logan's track record with the triplets' former nannies, one might argue that taking the job definitely put her in that category.

After she'd helped Jesse bundle the girls into their snowsuits the night before, Lori told him that she'd be there by six-thirty the next morning. She didn't know much about ranching but assumed Jesse's day started at sunup. The mixture of relief and gratitude in his eyes told her that she'd guessed correctly.

Fortunately, Lori had the day off from her job at the hospital, which would give her time to contact the personnel department at the hospital and talk to Janet, her supervisor.

Another factor that had proven God was at work in the situation. In fact, the longer Lori had thought and prayed about it, the more she realized that seemingly small and insignificant details now looked like signposts, directing her down a different path than the one she'd been on.

She wouldn't have known Jesse was looking for a nanny if Nicki hadn't called and asked for her help in the church nursery the night before. And just last week, Lori's landlady mentioned her niece had moved back to High Plains and needed a place to stay. She asked if Lori wanted to renew her lease, which was due the second week in December. Lori had told her that she planned to stay—but the lease agreement remained on her desk, still unsigned. Lori couldn't help but think that her landlady would be happy to offer the unit to a family member.

Even if Lori believed in coincidences—which she didn't—it would have been impossible to ignore the verse she'd read during her devotional time—the one she'd memorized while packing her suitcase. The one she silently repeated as she wove through a maze of baby jumpers and followed Jesse to the second floor.

A spacious landing opened up at the top of the stairs, and Jesse turned down the hallway to the left.

"You can have the room that adjoins the nursery." His husky voice dropped to a whisper as he nudged the door open.

Lori braced herself, ready to pretend to be enthusiastic.

Only, this time she didn't have to pretend.

The color scheme was a serene combination of subdued ivory, sage-green and a vibrant shade of blue that reminded Lori of Jesse's eyes....

The sky, she quickly corrected the errant thought. It reminded her of the *sky.*

She ventured farther into the room, aware that Jesse had put her suitcase down and moved aside to allow her to explore.

A queen-size antique four-poster bed, covered by a double wedding-ring quilt, dominated the room. Hand-hooked wool rugs had been strategically placed in front of the matching nightstands and the window. All places where bare feet might linger.

A sepia-toned photo of a man and woman held a prominent place on the wall above the headboard. Instead of staring somberly at the camera, typical for photographs taken during that era, the young couple was smiling at each other.

"My ancestors, Will and Emmeline Logan." Jesse stood beside her and Lori's heart did that crazy skip-hop thing again. "Will and Zeb Garrison founded High Plains in 1858, and Will married Emmeline a few years after that."

Lori forced herself to concentrate on the photo instead of the appealing, masculine scent of the man standing beside her.

More than a hundred years separated the two men, and yet the family resemblance was uncanny. Will Logan had the same bone structure—angular jaw and deep-set eyes—but his smile held a hint of mischief. "Was it your great-grandfather who started the Circle L?"

Jesse nodded. "He built the house for Emmeline. The ranch has been run by one of their descendants ever since."

Lori felt a stab of envy. What would it feel like to be part of such a strong family line? To share a legacy that had bonded its members together for more than a hundred years?

Her own family had splintered and fallen apart the summer after Lori had graduated from high school.

"It's beautiful," she murmured. "You must feel very blessed."

"Not everyone would agree with your opinion." Jesse pivoted sharply on his heel. "I'll show you the rest of the house and then I have to get to work. Clay is probably already in the barn waiting for me."

Lori found herself staring at his retreating back.

Not everyone would agree...

Agree with what? That his home was beautiful—or that he'd been blessed?

The headache that had anchored its claws in the back of Jesse's skull during the night finally worked its way around to his temples.

He hadn't expected Lori Martin's innocent questions to bring back an avalanche of memories…and regrets.

Marie had never described the house as beautiful. The first time she visited she labeled it "quaint," and Jesse, who'd taken it as a compliment, remembered thanking her. But several months after the wedding, she'd complained the rooms were too small and she felt cramped without adequate storage space. Without discussing it with him first, she'd talked to her father. Philip not only had an architect draw up a new blueprint, but then generously offered to pay the expenses so they could build something more suited to their style.

What Marie didn't understand was that the ranch *was* Jesse's style.

And he thought it had been hers.

Memories lapped against the walls Jesse had shored up around his heart.

The truth was, both of them had assumed a lot about each other.

They'd met at a rodeo, when Marie had come to town on what she described as a "girls' getaway" weekend. She sat down next to Jesse on the makeshift bleachers, her eyes sparkling with mischief as she told him that her friends had dared her to kiss a cowboy.

Unable to resist her charming smile, Jesse planted his favorite Stetson on Marie's head and kissed her on the cheek instead, surprised at his own boldness.

They had dinner that evening. And the next.

Marie extended her weekend stay to an entire week. When she finally left, she took Jesse's heart with her. After more than ten years of pouring his heart and soul into making the ranch a success, he'd been ready for someone to share it with.

Jesse had always been the levelheaded one when it came to life and relationships, but in spite of Maya's reservations, he proposed to Marie on Valentine's Day and they married less than six months later.

Unfortunately, it hadn't taken long for Jesse to realize that Marie had a romanticized, Hollywood view about life on a ranch. Emergencies ignited like brush fires, and as the owner of the Circle L, it was Jesse's responsibility to put them out. Night or day. Marie started to resent the hours he spent apart from her. She resisted Maya's attempts to befriend her, and refused to become part of the tight-knit community, but still complained that she was bored.

Bitterness scoured the lining of Jesse's stomach. He'd opened his heart and taken a risk. And in the end he'd lost.

He didn't blame Marie, he blamed himself. He'd written a fairy tale of his own—one in which he and his wife would work side by side during the day and sit together on the porch swing in the evening, waiting for the first star to appear in the sky. They'd laugh together. Raise a family together. The way his parents had.

But the reality? More arguments than laughter. And too many nights when Jesse had sat on the porch swing alone while Marie sat inside watching television or talking on the phone.

He didn't feel *blessed.*

"Mr. Logan? Jesse?" Lori Martin stood beside him, concern reflected in the depths of her amber eyes. "Is something wrong?"

Jesse's lips twisted.

Maybe she was worried that she'd agreed to work for someone who was losing his mind. Not that Jesse blamed her. A few times over the past few months, he'd wondered about that himself.

He frowned as his gaze dropped to the constellation of pale cinnamon freckles dotting the bridge of Lori's nose.

Funny, he hadn't noticed them until now.

With a jolt, Jesse realized he hadn't noticed how young she was, either. Probably in her mid-twenties. Her smile seemed to appear without warning or reason, and the lively sparkle in her eyes was evidence of a life that hadn't been touched by disappointment.

Lucky her.

Lori's response to his bluff the night before, when he offered and she accepted the nanny position, had left him stunned. It wasn't until Jesse watched her car glide up the driveway that he let himself believe she'd really accepted the position. And even then, he half expected to see her do a U-turn and hightail it back to town.

He'd stopped asking God for help a long time ago, but if Jesse didn't know better, he'd be tempted to think He was still looking out for him anyway.

Lori felt her face grow warm and she shifted uncomfortably under Jesse's intense perusal. Had her mascara smeared? Did she have a smudge of grape jelly on her nose?

An unhappy squawk on the other side of the door saved her from having to ask.

She and Jesse instinctively turned toward the sound.

"Brooke." They said the name at exactly the same moment.

Lori grinned at the expression on Jesse's face and she shrugged. "She's always the first one awake and ready to eat in the morning."

A shadow darkened Jesse's eyes. "I keep forgetting that you...know them."

Know them. Love them. Had even held them in her arms before Jesse....

Lori decided those thoughts were best kept to herself as she stepped into the nursery to say good morning to the girls.

She blinked, giving her eyes a moment to adjust to the shock.

Someone had painted the room...pink. But not a delicate, seashell-pink. A bright, vibrant, sensory-overload shade of Post-it Note pink.

But aside from the color of the walls and the identical white cribs lined up against the wall, it didn't look like a nursery.

No pictures on the walls. No mobiles over the cribs. The windows lacked curtains and, other than the beds, there wasn't a stick of furniture. Not even a rocking chair.

Lori's gaze moved to an enormous cardboard box positioned under the window. She decided it didn't count.

A sudden noisy chorus rose from the direction of the three cribs, and Lori no longer had time to dwell on the décor. Or lack thereof.

"When one wakes up, they all wake up." Jesse shook his head. "I stopped setting my alarm a few months ago— it seemed a little unnecessary."

Lori went to Sasha first, even though the baby wasn't exercising her lungs the way Brooke was. She'd captured her toes and was studying them with the same serious, intense expression Lori had seen on Jesse's face. She reached into the crib and Sasha's dimpled hand closed around her finger.

"Good morning, sweetheart. How did you sleep?" She glanced at Jesse. "Do you have a changing table somewhere?"

"It's in the box," Jesse muttered.

The box under the window.

Madison rolled over to watch the show, her thumb tucked firmly in her mouth. Lori blew her a noisy kiss. "Patience, sweet pea. I'll get to you in a minute."

Out of the corner of her eye, Lori saw Jesse's scowl.

It occurred to her that, if he'd fired someone for the songs she'd sung to the girls, maybe kisses were against the rules, too.

Not on *her* shift.

She'd spent hours caring for babies, and she knew that the more stimulation they received—the more people who touched and spoke to them—the more they thrived.

"If you have work to do, I can take it from here." And she'd be much less nervous if Jesse wasn't watching her.

Jesse hesitated.

"Really. We'll be fine." With Sasha in her arms, Lori breezed over to the changing table...*box*...and with one hand, flicked open a blanket before laying the baby down. She kept one hand on Sasha's tummy while reaching for a clean diaper from the stack on the floor.

Jesse hadn't taken the hint, and Lori felt the weight of his gaze as she deftly changed Sasha's diaper. It wasn't until *all* the babies had on fresh diapers that he finally retreated.

Lori sighed with relief.

"I must have made it through round one," she whispered to Madison.

The baby grinned.

"I know, I know." Lori winked at her. "I won't get cocky. Now, let's go down to the kitchen and find some breakfast."

And get ready for round two.

Chapter Four

"So, what do you think? Is this one going to work out?"

Clay's innocent expression didn't fool Jesse for a second.

He knew he should have followed his gut instincts. But no, in spite of his better judgment, he'd gone down to the barn and put himself in the crosshairs of Clay's wicked sense of humor.

As far as Jesse was concerned, the topic of the nannies that had come and gone over the past few months wasn't open for discussion. But if there was an invisible line drawn in the sand, his brother had to cross it.

"Time will tell." Jesse chose the safest response.

Clay rolled his eyes.

"She's very…calm," Jesse offered.

Really calm.

Lori hadn't seemed a bit rattled by the prebreakfast commotion. Jesse was always a little overwhelmed in the morning, when all three girls woke up within minutes of each other, bawling like newborn calves for their breakfast.

In his mind's eye, he saw Lori's lips purse as she blew

a kiss to Madison. He shook the image away, but another one—of Lori tickling the bottom of Sasha's tiny foot while Brooke wailed for her share of the attention—took its place.

"Patient," he added.

"That should work in your favor."

"I meant patient with the girls."

"Right. Sorry." Clay grinned. "And she didn't run screaming back to High Plains when she saw the living room. That's a good sign."

Jesse had thought so, too.

Not that he hadn't tried to keep up with the housework. And the laundry. And the cooking.

Even with two hired hands pulling ten-hour days and Clay coming onboard to help, Jesse had a difficult time staying on top of things at the ranch. It took every ounce of his energy to take care of the triplets in the evening and find a few free hours to work on the books. When he'd let the last nanny go two days before Tommy turned up missing, the house had taken a downward spiral.

Who was he kidding? Downward spiral? It had already hit bottom. Crashed and burned.

"I'm having dinner with Nicki so I won't be around this evening." Clay reached out and clipped Jesse lightly on the shoulder with his fist. "Lori sounds too good to be true. Don't mess this up."

"Me?"

"I've got two words for you: *five nannies*."

"I wasn't the problem." Jesse glared at his brother. "They weren't what I…expected."

The teasing sparkle in Clay's eyes faded. "Jess…" He paused, as if trying to find the right words. "You can't expect the girls' nanny to be like their…mother. It's not the same. It's not going to *look* the same."

His brother didn't realize the truckload of irony in that statement, Jesse thought. Marie hadn't wanted to be a mother. He'd watched her emotionally distance herself from the girls—the same way she had with him.

He had prayed. Back then. He prayed she would eventually come around. He prayed she would see the girls for the miraculous gift they were—but those hopes had been crushed when he found the note and her wedding rings that day.

A wave of bitterness swept through him. Belief in answered prayer. Hope. At one time, Jesse had had a surplus of both. But that was before he'd realized they left a lingering aftertaste of disappointment.

"I know this has been hard for you, Jess, but I'm here to help." Clay met his gaze. "Not just with the ranch but with…everything."

"Yeah, but for how long?" Jesse retorted.

As soon as he saw the shadow skim through his brother's eyes, Jesse silently berated himself.

"For as long as you want me to, whether you believe it or not." Clay's quiet promise weighted the air between them.

He sauntered out of the barn and Jesse closed his eyes.

What had happened to him?

Over the past six months, Jesse had been waiting for a sign that the well of bitterness inside of him was beginning to dry up. But instead, he felt as if it were constantly being replenished by an unknown source.

Maya told him that he had to let God work in his heart but Jesse wondered if he was beyond repair. Sometimes he thought the only thing that kept his heart beating was his daughters' sunny smiles.

She could *do* this.

Lori surveyed the living room and took a moment to regroup.

Triplets fed and dressed: check.

Laundry started: check.

Supper in the Crock-Pot: check.

Kitchen—

Lori winced. That room definitely fell under the promise: *I can do all things through Christ who gives me strength.* She planned to tackle that particular project while the girls took their morning nap.

After giving the triplets their bottles, Lori spread out a hand-pieced quilt on the floor of the living room and put all three babies in the center. While they worked their way to the edges, she deposited the toys into a large wicker hamper and sorted through the clothing draped over the swings.

Apparently, the men in the household had discovered a handy place to hang up their laundry after it came out of the dryer, saving the work of having to fold it and put it away.

Lori shook the wrinkles out of a faded denim work shirt and the subtle scent of sage and soap drifted into the air.

Jesse's.

She separated it from the stack of stylish, Western-style shirts that she had a hunch belonged to Clay Logan.

Lori didn't know Jesse's brother well, but he was engaged to her good friend and former neighbor, Nicki Appleton. She'd also seen him help rebuild the Old Town Hall, which had been leveled by the previous summer's tornado. He'd jumped into a battered old Chevy and took off down the road shortly after she'd arrived. And there'd been no sign of her new employer all morning.

She had no clue what the household routine involved, but the less contact she and Jesse had, the easier it might be to keep her job.

Unless…

"Uh-oh. Is there a nanny cam hidden somewhere, girls?" Lori anchored her hands on her hips and scanned the room, her gaze zeroing in on the only thing decorating the mantel above the stone fireplace—an unassuming silk fern.

"A tempting thought, but no."

The husky, masculine drawl sent a shiver chasing up Lori's spine, followed by a head-to-toe blush that probably turned her skin the same shade of red as her hair.

Lori whirled around. Jesse must have entered the house through an entrance other than the front door and snuck up on her.

"You're…here." *One point for your keen observation skills, Lori,* she chided herself.

Jesse shrugged off his duster and draped it over the back of the sofa. All three girls recognized their father's voice and immediately began to vie for his attention.

"It's ten o'clock," Jesse said.

Lori wondered if there was something significant about that particular time. Was she supposed to have lunch ready? The coffee on?

Or maybe Jesse performed daily inspections of his children and the nanny, like Captain Von Trapp in the movie *The Sound of Music.*

Now you're being paranoid.

"Ten o'clock," she repeated cautiously.

"I come in every day at ten."

"You're...finished for the morning?"

Jesse looked at her in disbelief. "Hardly."

So she'd been right. It *was* an inspection.

Lori took a deep breath. "I fed and dressed the girls. Supper is already in the Crock-Pot, but you didn't mention anything about lunch. You are a little low on groceries." She deliberately downplayed the sorry state of the refrigerator's contents. "So I will need to run to the grocery store within the next day or two. If there's something you'd like me to do right now—"

"You can go," Jesse interrupted.

Go?

Go as in *leave?* Return to her job at the hospital?

Lori looked down at the triplets and panic rushed through her.

She couldn't leave. The girls needed her. She wasn't sure what she'd done—or hadn't done—but somehow she'd broken the record for the shortest employment history with Jesse Logan.

"But what if I don't want to...leave?" There. She said it.

Jesse's eyebrow shot up. "I appreciate your dedication, Miss Martin, but I know how tiring taking care of the triplets can be. Put your feet up. Read a book. Take a walk. I don't care what you do, but the next half hour belongs to you."

Lori stared at him in disbelief. "You're giving me a *break?*"

Jesse sighed. "I'm trying, but you don't seem to be cooperating."

"But what about the girls?"

He gave her a wry look. "I think I can keep an eye on the girls."

Lori hesitated, still confused by his unexpected offer. "I have half an hour? To do anything I want to?"

"You are down to twenty-seven minutes now, but yes, that's generally the definition of a break."

Lori ignored the edge in his voice. "All right, then. I'll see you in twenty-seven minutes."

"Miss Martin?"

Lori sucked in a breath. Now what?

"You have…something…on your shirt."

Lori glanced down. So she did. A crusty river meandering down her shirt from collar to hem. Compliments of Brooke, who'd discovered a unique way of letting the person feeding her know when she was finished with her bottle.

"Thanks. I think."

"And your…foot."

Lori glanced down but couldn't identify what was spattered across the toe of her tennis shoe.

"Hazards of the job." Lori, who had experienced worse, couldn't help but smile. "And please, call me Lori."

Jesse didn't smile back.

It didn't matter, Lori decided, as she practically skipped across the living room.

She still had a job. And half an hour—well, twenty-seven minutes—would give her just the right amount of time to tackle one of the projects on her list.

Jesse's pulse settled back into its normal rhythm.

It was one thing to have Lori smile at his daughters, another to have her smile at *him*. And even with the remnants of Brooke's breakfast on the front of her shirt, she looked way too fetching.

Jesse pulled his unruly thoughts back in line.

Knowing how demanding the morning routine could be, he expected Lori would welcome a few minutes of alone time. But that wasn't the reason why, barring any unforeseen emergency on the ranch, Jesse had started the tradition of the ten o'clock break. It was important to give the nanny a break, but he also had his own, more selfish, reasons.

In order to get through the rest of the day, he needed to spend some time with his three favorite girls.

Jesse flopped down next to the quilt and carefully settled Sasha in the crook of his arm. His smallest daughter had gained weight over the past few months, but to Jesse, she still felt as fragile as spun glass.

When he brought Sasha home from the hospital, he'd been terrified to hold her—certain he'd either drop her or, worse yet, accidentally break her in half.

At the urging of the hospital social worker, he and Marie had taken a special class offered to the parents of preemies. The staggering amount of information hadn't put Jesse's mind at ease, but he'd waded through it anyway—never dreaming that in a few short weeks he'd be raising the triplets alone.

Jesse knew everything there was to know about ranching, but when it came to being a father, he felt completely out of his element.

As the months went by and the girls showed no signs of additional health complications, Jesse had relaxed a little. But, nanny or not, he still checked on them at least once during the night, and in the morning before he went out to start his chores.

Draping Maddie between his knees, Jesse watched Brooke wiggle away from him, intent on reaching one of the colorful toys scattered on the quilt.

His gaze swept the room again and he couldn't believe how much Miss Martin…*Lori*…had accomplished in just a few hours.

The room even *smelled* better. Like cinnamon and apples.

When he'd heard the sound of Lori's voice coming from the living room, he assumed she was on the telephone. But as he got closer, he realized she was talking to the girls. Hands planted on her slim hips, she'd been staring suspiciously at a fake fern and asking about a nanny cam.

The idea did have merit.

Modern technology like that would have come in handy when he'd discovered Nanny Number Three sound asleep on the couch while his hungry daughters wailed upstairs in their cribs.

Clay implied that he'd been too critical of the women he'd hired, but Jesse didn't know how he could be anything else. He worked long days, so the girls' caregiver would have an enormous influence on them. She had to be someone he could trust.

Someone like…Lori.

That he felt that way when he barely knew the woman surprised him. But there was something about her that instantly set her apart from the other nannies he'd hired. And fired.

Being an RN certainly qualified her to handle any medical emergencies that arose. She hadn't seemed upset by the fact that his daughters had decorated her clothing with their breakfast. And judging from the tantalizing smell filtering in from the kitchen, she knew how to make more than eggplant Parmesan.

And her smile…

He refused to think about her smile.

"We've got half an hour, ladies." Jesse turned his attention back his offspring. Much safer. "What would you like to do?"

In response to his question, Maddie began to gnaw on his knee and Sasha's tiny fingers closed around one of the buttons on the front of his shirt.

"Playtime. Got it."

For the next twenty minutes, Jesse let his world shrink to the size of the quilt spread out on the floor.

He cuddled Maddie, put together a chain of oversize plastic beads for Sasha and read a colorful cardboard copy of *Goodnight Moon* out loud. Three times.

Brooke had created a sport out of shedding her socks, so Jesse had to stop occasionally and wrestle them back on.

"It's footie pajamas for you tomorrow, Miss Logan," Jesse grumbled good-naturedly as he set Brooke in his lap once again and retrieved the tiny sock she'd discarded on her quest to reach the stuffed octopus Maya had bought as a coming-home present for the girls.

Brooke decided to protest the loss of her freedom and started to whimper. Like a chain reaction, Madison joined in, and then Sasha.

"You, too, sunshine?" Jesse reached for Sasha, whose forehead crumpled as she burrowed against his chest.

"If the three of you don't cheer up, You Know Who has to step in." Jesse eased Sasha out of his arms and laid her on the quilt next to her sisters.

The chorus picked up intensity.

"All right. You asked for it." Picking up the pink blanket an elderly member of High Plains Community Church had made for the girls, Jesse draped it over his head. "Don't say I didn't warn you. Here comes...*Flannel Man.*"

He roared the words—the girls always seemed to appreciate the drama—and made a growling noise deep in his throat. Shaking his head, he set the tassels on the blanket in motion.

Madison and Sasha stopped crying immediately, but Brooke, always his toughest critic, remained the last holdout.

Jesse dropped down on all fours. "Brooke Emmeline Logan—do you dare to challenge Flannel Man?"

Brooke's excited response not only drowned out the rest of the sentence but threatened to shatter the glass in the windows.

Jesse groaned and rolled onto his side. "I surrender. I surrender. Flannel Man has been vanquished."

Brooke's victory shriek rattled the china in the cabinet.

Three happy babies. Mission accomplished.

He peeked out from under the tassels of the blanket, just to make sure, and saw a pair of tennis shoes. A pair of tennis shoes with a glob of *something* spattered across the toes.

Lori.

Chapter Five

The living room was directly below the nursery, and Lori had just finished straightening up when she heard the girls begin to fuss.

She glanced at the clock. Ten-thirty on the dot. Nap time.

The commotion downstairs escalated, and the sound of a low but distinctively masculine growl—followed by a piercing shriek—turned Lori's knees to liquid.

Was Jesse...*scolding*...the girls? For simply doing something that all babies did?

Automatically, her feet carried her out the door and down the stairs. As Lori rounded the corner and rushed into the room she saw Jesse.

At least she was pretty sure it was Jesse.

Someone lay stretched out on the carpet next to the babies. Twitching. With a pink blanket over his head.

"Flannel Man is vanquished!" Jesse's dramatic groan drew another decibel-loaded shriek from Brooke.

Flannel Man?

Lori clapped a hand over her mouth as she took in the

fascinating scene and ventured closer. Only Jesse's shadowed jaw was visible below a fringe of tassels.

Suddenly the tassels shook, his body stiffened and Jesse jackknifed into a sitting position.

"What is it?" He yanked the blanket off in one swift motion. Eyes as blue as star sapphires locked with hers, daring her to comment.

"It's been a half hour, so I thought I should…um, put the girls down for their nap now." Lori struggled to keep her expression neutral.

When they'd met the night before, she'd judged him to be an indifferent father, similar to the man who had raised her. And now she'd caught him *playing* with them. A silly, imaginative type of play which hinted that a sense of fun lurked below Jesse's serious exterior.

He rolled fluidly to his feet, anchoring his hands on his hips. The silky dark hair went every which way, and Lori fought a crazy, inexplicable urge to reach out and smooth the tousled strands back in place.

She shoved her hands into the front pockets of her jeans. *What. Are. You. Thinking?*

"A half hour?" Jesse shot a disbelieving look at the grandfather clock in the corner of the room and Lori could have performed a cartwheel when it backed up her claim and began to chime.

He crossed his arms. "Okay. Go ahead."

Lori recognized a test when she saw one. And a person with two arms and three babies to transport upstairs and put to bed definitely qualified.

Lori was tempted to ask if she could please deal with Flannel Man instead. He seemed a *teensy* bit more approachable.

Under Jesse's watchful eye, she put Madison in the portable playpen and bent down to scoop up Sasha and Brooke, settling one on each hip.

They immediately struck up an unhappy duet.

"I think they want Flannel Man to perform an encore." Lori chuckled.

Jesse didn't.

Okaay. No encores.

"I'll be right back for Maddie." Heart pounding in her ears, Lori took the girls upstairs and settled them into their cribs.

Without knowing the girls' naptime routine, Lori had to improvise. She found a floppy stuffed horse under Brooke's comforter and tucked it in the corner of the bumper pad where the baby could see it.

"Do you have a friend, too, Sasha? Where is she hiding?" Lori spotted the baby's pacifier, but there was no sign of a favorite toy.

"It's a white cat. On the floor under the crib."

Jesse stood several feet behind her, Madison sprawled in his arms, looking completely content.

Lori didn't know the household rules yet, but was tempted to create one of her own—Jesse had to leave his cowboy boots on when he came inside. At least the jingle of his spurs would warn her of his approach.

She reached out to take Maddie from him and settled the baby on her back in the crib. Even before Lori finished tucking the crocheted blanket around her, Maddie's eyes drifted closed.

"Thank you for bringing her upstairs." Lori kept her voice low so she wouldn't disturb the girls.

Jesse didn't answer and Lori followed the direction of

his gaze to the window. Or rather, to what used to be in the cardboard box *underneath* the window.

"You used your break to put the changing table together?"

Lori caught her breath as Jesse stalked across the room. Probably to inspect her work.

"The directions weren't that complicated. And it came with one of those little black toolie things." Lori decided not to mention the plastic bag of "spare" parts left over from the project.

Jesse cleared his throat and looked away. "Are you referring to an Allen wrench?"

Had he almost…smiled?

When Jesse's gaze cut back to her and Lori saw his shuttered expression, she decided she must have imagined it.

"I guess so." Belatedly, it occurred to her that maybe she'd overstepped her boundaries. Or insulted him. After all, the changing table had sat unassembled for months, and she'd put it together in less than an hour. "I hope you don't mind, but you said I could use the time to do whatever I wanted."

For a few seconds the only sound in the room was the soft, rhythmic sound of the girls' breathing.

"I meant to get to it." Jesse sounded distracted as his hand traced the decorative edge of the wooden rail. "The tornado took out half the kitchen when it came through. I had to deal with that first."

His fingers closed around the rounded corner post and Lori noticed a thin band of white bisecting the sunwashed skin at the base of his ring finger.

The place where his wedding band had been.

Her heart clenched. Jesse had had so much to bear over

the past few months. Marie Logan's death—the single fatality from the tornado—had hit the close-knit community hard, but Nicki had hinted that Jesse repeatedly rebuffed offers from people to help.

"It takes time to rebuild," Lori offered quietly. "To put things back together."

Jesse's teeth flashed but it couldn't be classified as a smile. "Some things are never the same."

"The same, no," Lori agreed without thinking. "But God has the power to make something new."

"I'm sure you speak from experience." Jesse's cynical tone implied just the opposite.

Lori bit her lip. She *did* speak from experience, but sensed Jesse would argue that her loss couldn't compare to his.

Maybe it didn't look the same, but she understood what it was like to move forward into an unknown future and trust that God would be there every step of the way.

The girls need a father who loves You, Lord. A father who believes that You can be trusted no matter what happens in their lives....

"I won't be able to come in for lunch today, but we can discuss the specifics of your job after supper," Jesse said abruptly. "I have to get back to work now."

Lori watched him stride from the room and a piece of her heart went with him.

It was becoming clear that the trials Jesse experienced had eroded the foundation of his faith. In his anger, he'd chosen to walk away from the only one who could heal the wounds of the past. He doubted that God loved him.

Lori briefly closed her eyes.

She understood that, too.

* * *

Jesse slipped into the house through the back door and took a detour to the laundry room.

So much for good intentions.

`He'd promised Lori they would sit down together and go over the list of her responsibilities, but an emergency came up. He'd spent half the night in the barn, delivering a premature calf. Most of the fall calves had been born already, but a rancher could always count on having a few mamas who didn't do things by the book.

By the time Jesse discovered the cow in distress, the hired hands had already left for the day and Clay was on his way to High Plains to spend the evening with Nicki. Leaving Jesse to play midwife alone.

After several hours spent alternating between cheerleader and drill sergeant, he'd helped the exhausted mother bring a tiny but perfectly formed calf into the world.

Shrugging off his coat, he caught a glimpse of his reflection in the mirror above the laundry sink. Silently, he tallied up the damage. Hair damp with sweat, smudges of dirt on his face and bloodshot eyes. He didn't exactly smell like a red rose, either.

"I hate to say it, but that calf looked better than you do," Jesse told his reflection.

Fumbling with the buttons on his denim shirt, he stripped down to his T-shirt and tossed the offensive piece of clothing into the washing machine before Lori discovered it.

When he'd shown up for his morning play date with the girls, he noticed the clothes hanging on the baby swings had been folded and separated into three piles.

Another duty Lori had taken on that she shouldn't have.

Jesse didn't expect her to take care of everyone's laundry. He and Clay were big boys and could fend for themselves when it came to things like that. Something he would have brought up for discussion if they'd had the opportunity to talk.

Unfortunately, he hadn't been back to the house since Lori caught him—no, caught *Flannel Man*—surrendering to three seven-month-old babies.

The memory of being caught with a pink blanket on his head made Jesse wince.

So maybe it wasn't a game stamped with the official seal of parental approval, but he'd found out that whenever Flannel Man made an appearance, his daughters' tears miraculously dried up.

That was good enough for him.

But the sound of Lori's laughter when she'd teased him about the girls wanting an encore had lingered in Jesse's memory all day, like the melody of a song he couldn't get out of his head.

He turned on the faucet and cupped his hands under the stream of hot water, letting it wash away the blood stains and thaw out the joints in fingers stiff from the cold.

No matter how patient Lori seemed to be, Jesse doubted he was at the top of her list of favorite people now. After all, he'd hired her on the spot, without taking time to outline her duties, and then proceeded to abandon her—and his children—for the next ten hours.

And he'd skipped dinner.

If she thinks she's going to be responsible for everything around here, she'll be the first nanny you won't have to fire. She'll walk out the door all on her own.

Jesse dried his hands off on a towel and a familiar tightness constricted his chest as he made his way down the hall to the kitchen, hoping to scrounge up some leftovers.

The contractor he hired after the tornado had done a meticulous job reconstructing the kitchen, but Jesse still couldn't enter the room without reliving that day and the events that followed.

Since then, he avoided it as much as possible, choosing to eat meals in his office or on his way out the door. The room, once his favorite place to linger, now only served as a visible reminder of the things he'd lost.

His mother, Sara Logan, had always referred to the kitchen as "the heart of the home." Looking back, Jesse knew there had to have been some truth in that, because even though the old-fashioned parlor had been converted into a spacious, formal dining room before Maya was born, the entire family congregated in the kitchen instead.

It was there that Sara had created a welcoming oasis guaranteed to appeal to a weary husband, two growing boys and one horse-crazy daughter. They'd turn up there at various times throughout the day, lured in by the aroma of home-baked bread or a plate stacked high with crispy, paper-thin sugar cookies. The birds in the apple tree outside the window provided soothing background music. And more often than not, their mother would be sitting at the table when they came inside. Ready to talk…and listen.

When Jesse lay in bed at night, he could hear the soft murmur of his parents' conversation as the kitchen table became the connecting point between their days.

Every memory Jesse had of his mother was linked to the kitchen. Sara Logan's *heart of the home* had been a reflection of *her* heart. But in less time than it took to bridle a horse, the tornado had reduced it to a pile of stone and timber.

"An act of God."

Wasn't that what people called a tornado? Lori had sounded so convinced that God was in the business of rebuilding, but hadn't He been responsible for the storm's devastation in the first place? Jesus had calmed the winds once before—why had He turned his back on High Plains that day?

Why did He turn His back on me?

Jesse's footsteps slowed. Maybe he should skip the leftovers and spend an hour or two going over the budget instead. He remembered he'd left a jar of peanuts on the desk. If Clay hadn't gotten to them first.

"Jesse?"

Lori emerged from the kitchen and Jesse's thoughts scattered in a dozen different directions.

Dressed in loose-fitting gray sweatpants and a yellow T-shirt, she'd taken the braid out of her russet hair and it skimmed her shoulders like a glossy curtain.

How Lori managed to look as fresh and perky as she had when he'd seen her earlier that day was a complete mystery. In contrast, Jesse knew he looked as if he'd been forced through his grandmother's antique wringer washer. Backward.

"I thought you'd be asleep by now." Jesse couldn't help it that the words came out low and gritty, sifted through the gravel that suddenly filled his throat.

"You didn't come in for supper."

Jesse searched Lori's eyes, looking for signs of resentment as he braced himself for what would happen next. Lori would plead temporary insanity for giving up an eight-hour workday for a job with an absentee employer who required her presence 24/7. And expected her to cook, too.

And then didn't bother to show up for supper.

"I had to help a nervous mama deliver a calf." It was the truth, but as far as excuses went, Jesse figured Lori wouldn't accept it as a legitimate one.

Cows dropped calves all the time without assistance, but when that first-time mama had bellowed and rolled confused, mournful eyes in his direction, Jesse didn't have the heart to abandon her.

"I can understand that." Lori quickly corrected the statement with a soft laugh. "Oh, not the calf part. The nervous mama part."

The sound of her laughter blew holes in Jesse's defenses. Which explained why a few seconds later he found himself standing in the kitchen. A different kitchen than the one he'd been in that morning.

Lori hadn't simply straightened up the kitchen; she'd transformed it.

Jesse instantly recognized the lace tablecloth draped over the scarred surface of the oak table as one that his mother had used for company. Jesse's father had dabbled in woodworking and surprised her with the table as a gift for their tenth wedding anniversary.

The tornado had snapped off two of the legs, but Jesse couldn't bring himself to add it to the pile of debris. Instead, he'd hammered it back together and returned it to its rightful place in the center of the room.

His gaze lingered for a moment on the candle that served as a centerpiece before moving to Lori, who stood at the counter dishing up something from the Crock-Pot.

"My favorite thing about one-pot cooking is that the food doesn't dry out, even if you can't get to it right away."

To Jesse's astonishment, Lori handed the plate to him. The tantalizing aroma of roast beef, red potatoes and baby carrots made him forget all about the bowl of peanuts on his desk.

He stood rooted to the floor until he felt the touch of Lori's hand under his elbow, guiding him to the table. She clucked her tongue.

"Sit down before you fall down, cowboy."

Chapter Six

Lori wasn't sure what shocked her more, her boldness or the fact that Jesse obeyed.

Needing a few moments to compose herself, she left him sitting at the table and made a beeline for the coffeepot. Her hands trembled as she topped off one cup and poured a fresh one for Jesse.

She'd bathed the triplets and put them down for the night. Cleaned up the kitchen. Stashed a breakfast casserole in the refrigerator for the next morning.

Everything had been under control—except, she acknowledged ruefully, her emotions.

"Are you sure you want to do this, Lori? Jesse Logan reminds me of a dog with its leg caught in a trap—so focused on his own pain that he snaps at the people trying to help him."

Lori winced as the conversation she'd had with her former supervisor at the hospital scrolled through her memory. Janet Novak didn't believe in sugarcoating the truth, but Lori had always appreciated the fact that her boss was brave enough to speak it.

They'd talked on the phone shortly after the triplets had fallen asleep for the night. Janet was reluctant to accept her resignation, and asked Lori to consider using two weeks of her accumulated vacation time to determine whether she really wanted to give up her position at the hospital to be a full-time nanny.

Janet had also expressed reservations about the stability of the position and how Marie's death seemed to have changed Jesse. But instead of stirring up more doubts over the decision, her supervisor's caution only strengthened Lori's resolve.

After witnessing the way Jesse had playfully entertained his daughters that morning, Lori wanted to believe that below the painful experiences—the ones that had hardened like layers of sediment over Jesse's heart—was a man who could find hope again.

Until that happened, she would be there to love and care for the babies. And to pray.

But none of those things, she knew, explained why she waited up for Jesse to come in.

While restoring order to the kitchen, Lori tried to convince herself that she'd stayed up because she needed a clear definition of what was expected of her. More information about the triplets' schedule, pertinent details regarding directives from their pediatrician, special instructions.

But all it took to decimate her confidence was the sound of his footsteps in the hall.

And coming face-to-face with him?

More mustangs.

Beads of water clung to the tips of his tousled, dark hair, and glistened on the shadowed jaw, evidence he'd taken off the top layer of grime in the laundry room. In faded jeans and a plain white T-shirt that molded to the contours of his muscular torso, Jesse could have stepped off the cover of *Today's Cowboy*.

"Cream or sugar?" Lori waited until she was fairly certain her voice wouldn't come out in a squeak.

"No." Jesse paused. "Thank you."

The husky rumble of appreciation in his voice restored some of Lori's courage. She pulled out the chair opposite him and sat down. "You're welcome."

Their eyes met across the table and held for a moment until Jesse looked away.

The silence should have been uncomfortable, but for some reason, it wasn't. Maybe because Jesse tucked into his dinner with a masculine enthusiasm that made Lori glad she'd followed her instincts and put the roast in the Crock-Pot that morning.

"So…?" Jesse cleared his throat. "How did it go today?"

"Great."

"Great?"

"You sound surprised. What haven't you told me?" Lori grinned.

"Just about everything," Jesse muttered.

Lori figured that was as close to an apology as she was going to get. It would do for now.

"I understand emergencies," she said quietly. "They're a fact of life in the NICU. Let's consider today a practice run and start over tomorrow."

Jesse's chair suddenly scraped against the floor and his knee bumped the table, causing the flame of the candle to dance. "Thank you for keeping supper hot for me. It's been a long day, so maybe we should hold off on our meeting until tomorrow morning."

Jesse deposited his dishes in the sink and was on his way out the door before she had time to protest.

Lori had the strangest feeling he was running away.

But from what?

"Made it through the night, did you?" Jesse knelt down in the straw, mindful that Mama Cow had taken a protective stance over her calf. "Hey, I'm the one who helped you bring her into this world. Remember?"

Curious, the calf took a few wobbly steps closer, stretched out its neck and lipped Jesse's sleeve.

"Sorry." Jesse chuckled. "Breakfast is served over there." He tried to gently disengage the calf's mouth, but the touch of his hand spooked the tiny animal. It kicked up its heels and bolted.

Similar, he thought ruefully, to the way he'd responded the night before. He'd expected Lori to be angry that he hadn't kept their appointment. He hadn't expected…understanding.

Or a plate of hot food.

Sit down before you fall down, cowboy.

Lori's gentle humor had made it sound as if they shared a common purpose. That they were teammates rather than opponents.

But Jesse had grown accustomed to being alone.

He'd also grown accustomed to the bone-deep numbness that had settled into his soul and formed a seal around his heart after Marie's death.

Once Jesse had suffered a mild case of frostbite. When the feeling began to return to his fingers, the pain had been excruciating.

He'd relived the experience the night before.

For the first time since the tornado, he hadn't broken out into a cold sweat when he entered the kitchen—or been bombarded with painful memories. Instead, he'd felt enveloped in its warmth…and in the warmth of Lori's presence.

Let's consider today a practice run and start over tomorrow.

The trouble was, Jesse didn't know if he *wanted* to start over. And he didn't want to look too closely at the reason why.

If that made him a coward, Jesse could live with that.

He skipped breakfast, sent Clay out to feed the cattle and started the morning chores, but at five minutes to ten, cowardice was no longer an option.

The phone started ringing when he walked into the house, so Jesse took a detour into his office to answer it. "Logan."

"This is Toby at Anderson Furniture Gallery—"

"You must have the wrong number."

The man must have sensed he was a split second away from talking to dead air. "Wait a moment! Is Lori Martin there?"

Of course she was, but Jesse had no idea where. Come to think of it, the house was unusually quiet. "I can take a message."

"Wonderful." Toby's relief was palpable. "Please tell her there is a fifty-dollar charge for deliveries outside the city limits."

"Delivery charge for what?" Belatedly, it occurred to Jesse that it really wasn't any of his business.

"Ms. Martin called yesterday to inquire about purchasing a rocking chair."

Jesse frowned. "I'll pass that on and have her call you back."

"Thank you, sir, and have a great—"

The phone clattered back in its charger.

A rocking chair?

As Jesse stepped out of his office, a bansheelike cry above his head pierced the silence.

Brooke.

He took the stairs two at a time and turned left when he reached the landing.

"Don't cry, sweetie."

Jesse's footsteps slowed.

Once Brooke started the waterworks, trying to stop them was like trying to prevent a river from overflowing its banks. His eldest daughter's penchant for drilling holes in peoples' eardrums was the reason why he'd let Nanny Number Four go.

He'd come in earlier than usual one morning to make a phone call and heard Brooke raising the roof. Knowing she'd been fussy during the night, Jesse immediately went to investigate and make sure everything was all right. Halfway to the nursery, he heard the nanny respond with a harsh imitation of Brooke's wail followed by several seconds of scolding.

By the time he reached the top of the stairs, Sasha and Madison had joined in.

Two hours later, Nanny Number Four moved out.

"Brooke…honey. It's all right."

Brooke's wail reached a crescendo, and Jesse peeked into the room, not sure what he'd see.

The sight in front of him wrenched out a smile before he could prevent it. Lori sat in front of Brooke's infant seat, waving her arms, the upper half of her body shrouded by a blanket.

"Look, sweetie. Here's...*Flannel Man.*"

Since the blanket didn't muffle the feminine, musical sound of Lori's voice, Jesse knew there would be no fooling the small audience watching her. Especially Brooke.

"Identity theft is a crime, you know."

At the sound of Jesse's voice, Lori wanted to scuttle into the closet and hide. If the man had fired a nanny for singing the "wrong" songs to the triplets at bedtime, her job was definitely on the line for impersonating a superhero.

She lifted the corners of the blanket and peeked out.

And saw Jesse...smiling.

Lori blinked several times to be sure. Just in case the blanket covering her head had somehow temporarily cut off the flow of oxygen to her brain and affected her vision.

No. Still smiling. An irresistible smile that softened the stern jaw and deepened the blue of his eyes to the color of a summer evening sky.

Her heart somersaulted in her chest as Jesse sauntered into the room. Lori would have stood up but had a hunch that her knees wouldn't support her. They felt a little... spongy.

But who could blame them?

After Jesse's abrupt departure during their conversation the night before, Lori had gone to bed wondering if she was on shaky ground. When she'd made her way to the kitchen to mix up the girls' bottles that morning, she discovered a note taped to the refrigerator. Evidence that Jesse had decided to save himself the time and trouble of an actual face-to-face meeting and condense her duties onto a three-by-five card instead.

"Giving Lori a hard time this morning, princess?" He knelt down in front of Brooke, whose tears evaporated like water on a hot skillet at the sight of her daddy.

"I was doing fine until you blew my cover," Lori muttered, rising to her feet with as much dignity as she could muster.

"It wouldn't have worked anyway." Jesse's words stopped her dead in her tracks as she made her way to the door. "You were missing Flannel Man's secret power source."

Lori turned around.

Was Jesse teasing her? It was difficult to tell, given the fact that his heart-stopping smile had come and gone as quickly as a shooting star.

She moistened her lips. "Secret power source? And what would that be?"

Jesse shrugged. "A secret."

Lori shook her head.

Of course it was.

"Something smells delicious. Any chance I can try a sample?"

Lori chuckled at Clay Logan's hopeful expression as she took a pan out of the oven. "It's nothing fancy—just peanut butter brownies. The roast chicken is for supper tonight."

"Dessert?" Clay clapped his hand over his heart and pretended to stagger into the kitchen. "Roast chicken? Let me tell you something, Miss Lori. After two weeks of living on hamburgers and beans, that sounds pretty fancy to me."

Lori couldn't help but be warmed by the praise. Somewhere along the line, Clay had learned the importance of positive feedback.

Unlike Jesse. When it came to the eldest Logan brother, Lori was beginning to think that *not* being fired meant she was doing a good job.

"I found a box of recipes in the cupboard, and I hoped this one was a favorite." Lori nodded toward the decorative tin on the countertop, the one she'd accidentally stumbled upon during a quick inventory of the kitchen the day before.

The majority of the recipes were handwritten on traditional recipe cards, but several had been jotted down on scraps of paper.

"That looks like Mom's." Clay's smile faded slightly. "But I'm surprised Maya didn't take it when she moved into town after..."

His voice trailed off and the flash of pain in his eyes revealed an old hurt, leaving Lori at a loss for what to say.

"Maybe Maya didn't know the box was there," she suggested cautiously. "It was buried pretty deep in the back of the cabinet."

She hadn't lived in High Plains long enough to know all the details of his family history, but the night she'd volunteered in the nursery, Nicki had mentioned the Logans' parents had died together in a car accident years ago.

Oddly enough, although Clay was the one standing in front of her, Lori felt a rush of compassion for Jesse. He lost both parents and his wife...and for several days after the triplets' birth there'd been a question whether or not Sasha would survive.

No wonder the man's heart had gone into lockdown.

Unaware of her turbulent thoughts, Clay picked up the tin and his thumb grazed a trail over the top of the cards. A faint smile lifted the corners of his lips.

"When I was about six or seven, I remember Mom asking Grandma Logan to write down her recipe for Christmas fudge. Gram insisted she didn't have one, so Mom followed her around the kitchen with a pen and pencil, taking notes while she made it. Dad and Grandpa rounded us kids up and herded us into the den to watch television." He gave a low laugh. "If I remember right, Dad's exact words were 'children should see a fireworks display at the Fourth of July celebration, not Christmas.'"

The thread of affection in Clay's tone made it clear the adults had seen the humor in the situation.

"You must have a lot of good memories growing up here." Lori smiled wistfully. Over the past few years she'd come to accept that her own memories of "Christmas past" were best left there—in the past.

Clay's smile widened. "I remember the year we got a toboggan for Christmas. Mom and Dad had two rules. Rule one: no fighting over it. Rule two: Jesse got to sit in front and steer the thing because he was the oldest."

"But you wanted to."

"Good guess." Mischief danced in Clay's eyes. "I waited until everyone was busy and took my chance. Except things didn't go quite the way I expected. My foot got caught in the rope and the sled flipped over. By the time I got to the bottom of the hill I had a sprained wrist and a bloody nose—"

"And you sneaked up the hill to try it again the next day."

Lori felt the sudden drop in temperature, as if someone had opened a window. She didn't understand the tension that suddenly crackled in the air but she recognized its source.

Jesse.

Chapter Seven

The stare down between the two men lasted so long that Lori wondered if she was supposed to declare a winner. Instead, she aimed a bright smile in Clay's direction.

"Points for perseverance," Lori said, keeping her voice light. "What happened then?"

Clay dragged his gaze away from Jesse and shrugged. "My big brother stopped me."

Jesse's expression darkened. "That time."

The tick of the clock on the wall sounded as loud as a shotgun blast in the split second of silence that followed the words.

"That time," Clay agreed softly.

What on earth is going on? Lori thought. She deliberately stepped between them to draw Jesse's fire. "Is everything okay upstairs? I was just about to check on you and the girls."

"I put them down for their nap already. They seemed a little out of sorts this morning."

Mmm. Kind of like someone else she knew.

Jesse's gaze cut back to his brother. "Did you need something?" He managed to turn the simple question into a challenge.

"The vet called to let you know the shipment of antibiotics you ordered is in." Clay's tone remained even, but his hands clenched at his sides. "I can go into town and pick it up this afternoon."

Lori recognized an olive branch when she saw one. But what did Clay have to apologize for?

"Fine," Jesse finally said.

No "thank you, Clay." No softening of that granite jaw. No flicker of warmth in his eyes.

Lori wanted to smack her hand against her head. Or his.

Discouragement battled her earlier optimism. When Jesse interrupted Clay's story, Lori had assumed the tension between the two brothers was the result of a recent difference of opinion or misunderstanding.

But now something told her that its roots went deeper into the past.

Lori knew from experience the influence a child's environment could have on his or her life. How it colored their perspective. Influenced the way they viewed others…and themselves.

He's so focused on his pain he snaps at the people who are trying to help him.

But did that include his own brother?

Clay set the recipe tin back on the counter and gave her a polite nod. "Lori. You're doing a great job, but be sure to let us know if you need anything."

"I will." It was nice to know someone was on her side.

Jesse's scowl deepened. He didn't budge when Clay reached the door, and, for a split second, Lori was sure the two men were going to collide. At the last second, however, Jesse shifted his stance and Clay brushed past him.

"Excuse me." Lori decided it would be wise to follow Clay's lead. Before she grabbed a chair from the kitchen table and put Jesse in a time-out for rude behavior.

Instead of moving to the side the way he had for Clay, Jesse stepped in her path, effectively blocking her escape.

Lori's nose twitched and she suppressed a smile, finding it difficult to be intimidated by a man who smelled like baby powder. Not that intimidation was Jesse's intent, but the man did have a talent for imitating a thundercloud.

"You had a phone call. Someone named Toby from the furniture store."

The rocking chair she'd inquired about. And Jesse had taken the call. It was too late to wonder if maybe—just maybe—she should have discussed the addition of a new piece of furniture with him prior to calling Anderson Furniture Gallery.

"I'll call him back later." She tried to inch around him, but Jesse's gaze pinned her in place.

"Why do you need another rocking chair? We already have one."

He had to be kidding.

Was it possible he really didn't have a clue why she wanted a rocking chair in the nursery?

Lori searched his expression and saw…confusion.

Okay, maybe it was possible.

"Yes, you do," she agreed. "But it's in the living room."

Jesse didn't respond, obviously waiting for the rest of the explanation.

Burying a sigh, Lori obliged. "If one of the triplets

wakes up in the middle of the night, I don't want to stumble all the way downstairs to rock her back to sleep."

Not to mention that said rocking chair was an enormous tweed rocker-recliner that looked as if it could easily swallow a hundred-and-fifteen-pound nanny whole. Or that she'd learned the hard way the night before that trying to slip out of the room to calm one baby somehow tripped an internal "triplet radar" that woke up the other two. Instead of comforting one baby, she'd had three to settle back down.

Jesse didn't look convinced.

"Is that what you usually do?" Lori made another valiant attempt to bridge the communication gap. "Bring them downstairs one at a time to rock them back to sleep?"

"No." Jesse tunneled his fingers through his hair and frowned. "They like to be boggled, not rocked."

"Boggled?"

A red stain worked its way up his neck and spread across his handsome features. "You know, a cross between a bounce and a…joggle."

Lori bit down on her lip to prevent a bubble of laughter from escaping. "Oh. Right. *A boggle.*"

"It works." Jesse crossed his arms.

Noting the defensive gleam in his eyes, Lori realized it probably wasn't the best time to point out that Sasha had been content to sit in her lap and rock for hours the night she'd helped Nicki in the church nursery.

But Jesse was the boss, and she was determined to break the nanny curse.

"I'm sure it does." Lori tamped down her disappointment. "And I'm sorry. I should have asked you about a rocking chair first. It won't be a problem to cancel the order."

"Is it fancy?"

Now it was Lori's turn to be confused. "Fancy?"

Jesse arched a brow. "The rocking chair?"

"Oh, no, not at all." Lori felt her freckles start to glow. "I saw it in the window display last week. It's maple, but it does have a pretty seat cushion." A horrifying thought occurred to her. Did Jesse think she was going to present him with the bill? "I don't expect *you* to pay for it, of course, because I'm the one who wanted—"

"There's a rocking chair up in the attic that belonged to my grandmother." Jesse cut through her rambling. "I can't guarantee what kind of condition it's in anymore, though."

"I'm sure it'll be fine." Lori tried not to let her excitement show. She had explored her new surroundings enough to be thoroughly charmed by the bits and pieces of Jesse's family history that added up to create a cheery warmth in his home. "Do you mind if I take a look?"

Jesse hesitated and then jerked his head toward the stairs. "Come on."

Now it was Lori's turn to balk. "I know you're busy. Just point me in the right direction and I'll find it."

"Indiana Jones would have a hard time finding it," he said dryly. "And I think I can spare a few minutes."

Jesse waited at the top of the landing while Lori took a quick peek at the triplets to make sure they were still asleep.

"We're good to go," she whispered, backing quietly out of the nursery.

Jesse gave a curt nod. "This way."

"This way" proved to be down the opposite hall and into a small bedroom.

It took Lori a split second to realize it belonged to

Jesse. With a pang of guilt, she realized he'd given up the larger bedroom so she could be closer to the triplets.

"The staircase leading to the attic is in the closet." Jesse opened the doors and disappeared inside. "I haven't been up there since…for a few years…so I have to move some boxes out of the way."

Lori took advantage of his absence to study the room.

The simple, masculine décor reflected the man she was beginning to know, from the neat stack of books on the nightstand to the shoes lined up against the wall.

Just as she suspected, everything served a purpose and was displayed in its rightful place…except for the collection of picture frames shaped like flowers sprouting from the top of his dresser.

The splash of primary colors against the dark woodwork was so unexpected that Lori paused to take a closer look.

Judging from the girls' smiling, dimpled cheeks, she guessed the photos had been taken within the past month. Fascinated, Lori's gaze drifted to a daisy-shaped frame. Each "petal" held a miniature photo of the girls, but in the center was a picture of Jesse sitting in a leather chair, all three babies fanned out on his lap. He wasn't smiling—naturally—but the photographer had captured the mixture of love and pride on his face as he looked down at his daughters.

One of the frames on the dresser had fallen over, and automatically, Lori reached out to stand it back up.

Her heart missed a beat as she found herself staring at a close-up of Jesse and Marie. It must have been taken on their wedding day, although the ornate altar and soaring stained-glass windows didn't look familiar.

But then again, neither did the couple in the photo.

Marie, dressed like a fairy-tale princess in an elaborate satin, beaded gown, smiled at the camera while Jesse stared down at his bride with an adoring expression. His rugged features looked carefree rather than wary, the blue eyes warm and unguarded.

What happened between them? Why did Marie leave?

The questions tumbled over one another in Lori's mind.

Her brief interactions with Jesse's former wife at the hospital had been disturbing—a hint into the heart and mind of a woman desperately unhappy with her life.

Lori couldn't understand why. Most of her dreams had revolved around having a family. A loving husband. Children. A welcoming home. All the things Marie Logan had chosen to walk away from.

A loud thump followed by a muffled groan jerked Lori back to reality.

"Someday I hope I get the chance to ask Will Logan what he was thinking when he designed the house." Jesse poked his head out of the closet a split second after Lori set the frame down. "I guess we're set."

Lori peeked into the closet just in time to see Jesse swipe away a skein of filmy cobwebs in the doorway above his head. She shuddered. Maybe the tweed rocker-recliner in the living room wasn't so bad....

"Watch your head." Jesse started up the steps, his broad shoulders barely clearing the narrow stairwell.

And the rest of me, Lori silently added, as one of the wooden planks bowed beneath her weight.

Jesse paused suddenly and twisted around to look at her. "Be careful when you get to the top. The last step is a bit of a challenge."

Lori looked past him and squinted into the shadows. "I don't see a…last step."

"That's why it's a challenge." Jesse's elusive smile flashed in the gloom.

Lori swallowed hard. Jesse's smile should be accompanied by a warning from the surgeon general. Twice in one day was about all her heart could take.

"You can do it. Take my hand." Jesse must have thought it was fear that kept her frozen in place, when his smile was to blame.

Lori took a deep breath as Jesse's fingers closed around hers. She felt the gentle scrape of calluses against her palm…and the little pulses of electricity that danced up her arm.

Jesse's breath hissed between his teeth.

Shaken, she wondered if he'd felt it, too.

As soon as Lori's feet connected with the floor, Jesse let go of her hand and stalked away. Lori willed her knees to keep her upright.

She couldn't be attracted to Jesse. God had brought her to the ranch for the triplets. To make sure they grew up knowing they were loved.

Jesse does *love his daughters.*

The thought swept in and Lori silently acknowledged the truth in it. The man could be as tough and unyielding as a piece of cold leather, but in the presence of those babies, Lori caught a glimpse of another side of him. A softer side.

But she hadn't thought of it as a *dangerous* side. At least not where she was concerned.

Until now.

Jesse couldn't look at Lori.

Not that *not* looking at her made a bit of difference.

Especially when the light floral scent she favored had followed him to the opposite corner of the attic. And every nerve ending in his body still tingled from the simple touch of her hand.

Jesse stifled a groan.

He didn't *want* to feel anything. Been there, done that—and had the open wounds to prove it. Even the people closest to him had lacked staying power—and there had to be a reason.

Who was he kidding? *He* was the reason.

"It looks like a flea market up here!"

Jesse heard Lori's muffled voice, but all he could see was the top of her head as she worked her way through the maze of discarded furniture and boxes. He dragged his gaze away from the gold threads the overhead light illuminated in her hair. He took a quick inventory of his surroundings and discovered that Lori was right.

Marie preferred a more contemporary style, so she had started to replace the contents of the house with more modern furnishings. Jesse had encouraged her, hoping she would feel more at home, but he hadn't realized until now how many things had been banished to the attic.

"I think I found it!" There was no mistaking the lilt of excitement in Lori's voice. "Come and look."

In order for Jesse to "look," he had to be closer to her. Which meant he had to stop hiding in the corner with the spiders.

Working his way over to Lori, he found her on her knees. Eyes shining as she used the hem of her shirt to brush away the dust coating the seat of a rocking chair.

He shook his head. "Wrong one."

"What do you mean?"

"I forgot about this one, but I'm pretty sure it came in on the wagon train with Emmeline. The family founders passed on the pack-rat gene, I'm afraid. We never get rid of anything."

"You shouldn't." Lori looked dismayed at the suggestion. "Oh, it's not the things themselves that are so important, but the stories they tell. They're connected to your family history, and as the girls get older, you'll be able to share the stories behind them." Her voice softened. "They won't have to struggle to figure out who they are and where they fit. They'll know."

If only it were that simple, Jesse thought. He wasn't even sure where *he* fit anymore.

He stared down at the chair, not wanting Lori to see how her words had affected him. She made it sound like a positive thing—sharing the Logan family history with his daughters.

What stories will you tell them? A mocking voice infiltrated his thoughts. *How about the night you and Clay argued and he left the ranch for good?*

He hadn't meant to eavesdrop on Clay and Lori's conversation in the kitchen, but when Jesse heard his brother putting a humorous spin on the toboggan incident, anger had welled up inside of him.

His perspective of that day differed a bit from his brother's.

Clay's little adventure with the sled and the subsequent trip to the emergency room had resulted in their parents' disappointment—with *him*. His mother and father never came right out and said it, but as the older, responsible one in the family, Jesse had been forced to shoulder the unwelcome burden of keeping his younger sibling out of trouble. Trouble that had only multiplied as Clay's spirited antics eventually spiraled into full-blown rebellion—and ultimately led to the tragedy that had cracked the foundation of their family.

Were those the stories he was supposed to pass on?

"Jesse?"

His skin jumped at the tentative touch of Lori's hand on his arm. But what stunned him even more was the compassion in her eyes—as if she could read his troubled thoughts. As if she *understood.*

But how could she? Lori hadn't experienced the devastating losses he had. She appeared to have a strong faith, but Jesse doubted it had been tested to the point where she felt as if she'd stumbled into a place beyond God's hearing. Beyond His reach.

A few weeks after the tornado struck High Plains, Jesse overheard a customer at the feed store admit that every time the sky clouded over he couldn't help but stare at the horizon. Waiting for the next funnel cloud to appear.

Jesse could relate. Only, he wasn't waiting for the next storm to arrive—he was waiting for the next person he cared about to leave.

Lori swallowed hard.

She'd touched Jesse. *On purpose.* Knowing he wasn't a man who sought out help or comfort.

Offering encouragement had been part of her job in the NICU but this felt different. This was…*Jesse.* Lori wanted to do something—say something—to coax him away from the ledge of dark memories that had drawn him in. To remind him that he wasn't alone.

Amazingly enough, it worked. The bleak look in

Jesse's eyes faded, replaced by a wariness that told Lori his defenses were back up and running. Now that she had his attention, she wasn't sure what to do with it!

"This rocking chair will be fine, don't you think?" She casually withdrew her hand from Jesse's arm—ignoring the current rocketing down to her toes—and set the chair in motion.

"It doesn't look very sturdy."

Lori's training kicked in, and while he watched, she gave the chair a brief but thorough examination. "One of the spindles is a little loose, but I should be able to glue it."

"Right." Jesse's expression was skeptical. "And you'd somehow manage to fit that in between taking care of the triplets, making home-cooked meals and restoring the house to its original state of disrepair."

Lori caught her lower lip between her teeth and peeked up at him from underneath her lashes. Guilty as charged. "You noticed that, huh?"

"I noticed."

He noticed, but it was difficult to tell from his expression whether or not he approved.

"According to the three-by-five card taped to the refrigerator, I do have some free time in the evenings," Lori reminded him. "And I have a ten o'clock break every morning…*and* Sundays off."

Jesse's eyes narrowed. "That's *your* time. To relax and regroup."

"Great." She gave him a sunny smile, dusted her palms against her jeans and reached for the rocking chair. "Because I find all those things you just mentioned *very* relaxing."

Chapter Eight

"**W**hat are you doing?"

Lori's foot slipped off the rung of the ladder. If the sound of Jesse's voice hadn't been enough to send her into cardiac arrest, the steadying touch of his hand against her leg a split second later packed enough power to finish her off.

Her breath stuck in her throat.

"I'm hanging up this…garland." The garland that had slipped out of her hand and drifted to the floor before she could finish threading it through the brass chandelier.

"That's funny. It looked to me like you were trying to break your neck," Jesse growled up at her.

The ladder *was* a bit rickety, but Lori wanted to argue she'd been doing just fine until he'd blown in like an early winter storm.

Early being the key word.

She'd hoped to have the house completely transformed by the time he returned. To surprise him.

Well, mission accomplished, Lori thought, as she delicately shifted her weight to regain her balance. Jesse did look surprised. Just not *pleasantly* surprised.

Something she should have gotten used to by now.

A week of living in Jesse's house had driven Lori to cross-stitch her "I can do all things through Him who strengthens me" verse from Philippians 4:13 on a bookmark she tucked in her bible. But as an extra reminder, she'd written it on a three-by-five card and taped it to the refrigerator—next to the one Jesse had put up outlining her duties!

The man was turning out to be a study in contradictions. Just when she thought she had Jesse figured out, he did something completely unexpected. Like offering a helping hand. Or smiling.

No matter how tired or preoccupied Jesse looked when he came into the house at ten o'clock every morning, when Lori showed up a half hour later, he seemed…rejuvenated. As if he needed the time with his daughters as much if not more than they did.

He would disappear into his office every evening after supper but reappear in time to help her bathe the triplets and get them ready for bed—something Lori hadn't expected when he'd hired her as a live-in nanny.

Ever since the day they'd gone up in the attic to find the rocking chair, she and Jesse, out of necessity, formed a tentative alliance. But every time their paths crossed, the interaction reminded Lori of the couples on those popular television dance competitions, who had to learn the steps of a new dance together. Sometimes the result was awkward. Sometimes humorous. And sometimes it was downright painful.

Considering the expression on Jesse's face, Lori had a feeling this was going to be one of the downright painful encounters. Because, once again, it looked as if she'd stepped on his toes.

"Could you please hand me that piece of garland?" Lori decided to bluff her way through. A misstep was only a misstep if a person couldn't recover quickly enough to make it look like part of the routine.

Jesse reached down and picked up the length of artificial balsam, studying it with the same suspicion he might a chunk of meteor he found smoking in the pasture. "Where did this come from?"

"I saw a box of Christmas decorations in the attic when we were looking for the rocking chair. Umm, where are the girls, by the way?"

Her pathetic attempt to distract him failed.

"Maya asked if she could keep them a few more hours. She's going to bring them back later this evening." His gaze broke away from her and zeroed in like a laser pointer on each new addition to the décor. The ceramic gingerbread village, with its miniature figurines that now populated the mantel. A hand-carved nativity scene on the coffee table. The old spinning wheel Lori had wrestled down the stairs and, in a burst of creativity, embellished with a spray of artificial holly berries.

She'd also started a fire in the fireplace, more to provide a welcoming atmosphere than to chase the chill out of the room.

Finally, Jesse's inventory was complete, and he looked up at her. "It's Sunday."

"Yes, it is." Lori knew that. She and Clay had driven into town together to meet Nicki and Kasey at High Plains Community for the morning worship service. Maya and Greg had been there, too, with Layla and Tommy in tow. Maya had mentioned that Jesse accepted her invitation to spend the afternoon with them, but Lori hadn't realized the triplets would be enjoying an extended visit with their aunt.

"Your day off," he added.

She knew that, too. It was on the three-by-five card. "Am I putting up the decorations too soon?"

"Too soon?" Jesse repeated the words. "No, what I meant to say was that it wasn't necessary."

"But…it's the triplets' first Christmas."

A shadow skimmed across Jesse's face before he averted his gaze. "They won't remember it. I didn't expect you to go to all this trouble."

Maybe the babies were too young to appreciate—or remember—their first Christmas, but that didn't stop Lori from wanting to make it special.

Her brave foray back to the attic reminded her a little of Christmas morning, yielding an incredible bounty of treasures buried inside those dusty boxes.

Along with the traditional glass balls, she'd discovered a box containing fragile handmade ornaments—three small handprints preserved in plaster of Paris. Each one had a name written on the back—Jesse, Clay and Maya. Underneath those, carefully protected by a layer of crisp paper snowflakes, was a team of clothespin reindeer, complete with pom-pom noses and toothpick antlers.

Not sure what to display, she'd made three trips up and down the stairs and brought everything down. And once she started unpacking boxes, it had been difficult to stop.

"It's no trouble," she said softly, tempted to add that she was looking forward to the days counting down to Christmas.

For the past few years, with nowhere to spend the holiday, she volunteered to take extra shifts. It gave her a sense of satisfaction to know that, in a small way, giving her time that way meant someone else would be able to spend Christmas with their loved ones.

But this Christmas would be different. It would be the kind of Christmas she'd always dreamed of. She'd already found several recipes she wanted to try—including the one for Grandma Logan's Christmas fudge—and she decided to wrap white lights and garland around the staircase banister.

"Still, I—"

"Special delivery!" A cheerful bellow drowned out Jesse, as Clay poked his head inside the door and grinned at Lori. "Seven feet tall. And as big as a round bale of hay."

"You brought a tree." In her excitement, Lori practically slid down the ladder....

And landed smack dab in the warm circle of Jesse's arms.

The top of Lori's head bumped against Jesse's chin. His arms automatically went around her slender frame as he put out one foot to keep his balance.

Too bad that only worked on the *outside*. Because Lori's unique fragrance—the one that reminded him of wildflowers—was already creating havoc on the inside.

"Sorry," Lori gasped, eyes wide as she twisted in his arms and stared up at him. "Are you all right?"

Not even close, Jesse thought as he silently willed his hands to let go of her.

Over the past week, he'd tried to maintain a safe distance between them, but he was beginning to suspect there was some kind of conspiracy to thwart that plan.

For one thing, all three of his precious daughters had taken to expressing their displeasure—rather loudly—

whenever Lori left the room. Not even Flannel Man could cheer them up. Jesse knew he should have been relieved the girls had bonded with their new nanny so quickly…if he also hadn't noticed they seemed to be the most content when he and Lori were *both* in the room with them.

And out of sheer necessity, he and Lori were together. A lot.

The triplets' presence at dinner kept everyone's attention focused on them, and after the meal Jesse could escape to his office or the barn. But later in the evening he and Lori joined forces to carry out what she had cheerfully dubbed the "three *B*s." *Baths, bottles and blankies.* Jesse would have described it as the hour and a half of absolute pandemonium that preceded the triplets being tucked into their cribs for the night.

That Lori was able to have a sense of humor about a challenging triathlon involving wriggling *wet* babies— followed by wriggling *hungry* babies—had made it even more difficult to maintain the safe distance that Jesse thought he needed to be, well…safe.

The kitchen Jesse had spent the past five months avoiding once again welcomed him when he stopped in for a break or to have lunch. But it wasn't just hot coffee and the promise of Lori's cooking that caused him to linger. He was becoming uncomfortably aware that lately he found himself looking forward to seeing Lori during the day.

No matter where Jesse went, he could hear the sound of her warm laughter flowing through the house, eroding his determination to keep their relationship strictly employer and employee.

It was one of the reasons he'd accepted Maya's invitation to spend the afternoon with her family and let Lori enjoy her day off—he wanted to make sure the boundaries were firmly in place. For his sake more than hers. But he hadn't expected Lori to use her afternoon off to transform his home into a Christmas wonderland.

"I can't believe you brought us a tree." Lori practically skipped across the room toward Clay. "I wasn't sure when I'd have a chance to drive into High Plains and get one."

"You can thank my fiancée. She mentioned the two of you had a long conversation about the perfect tree after church this morning. When we took Kasey to pick one out after church, Nicki saw this one and thought of you." Clay swept off his hat. "I would have been home sooner, but Greg, Reverend Garrison and I decided to volunteer at the Old Town Hall for a few hours."

Jesse waited for his brother to comment on the fact that he'd declined an invitation to join the work crew, but Clay just looked around the room and grinned. "Wow. You've been busy today, too. It looks great in here."

"Really?" Lori's smile bloomed and Jesse felt another hard pinch to his conscience. Instead of complimenting her efforts, he'd told her that she shouldn't have bothered. "I hope the decorations don't make the room look too crowded."

The corners of Clay's lips kicked up. "Nope—it reminds me of the way the house looked when we were kids. Mom pulled out all the stops at Christmas. Dad always teased her by saying she was trying to compete with the North Pole."

This was the second time Jesse had heard his brother fondly reminisce about their childhood and he couldn't believe how selective his brother's memory was. Had Clay conveniently forgotten all the Christmases he'd been a no-show after their parents had died, ignoring Maya's tearful pleas for him to come home?

"Well, where do you want the tree?" Clay sauntered into the room and propped his hands on his hips. "Are you planning to decorate it tonight?"

"I can't find the stand. It wasn't in the attic with the rest of the things."

"Jesse probably knows where it is."

Both Clay and Lori turned toward him, and Jesse tried unsuccessfully to steel himself against the avalanche of memories that Clay's little side trip down memory lane had triggered.

Growing up, Christmas had always been a big deal, but their parents had never let the busy pace and gift-giving get buried under the real reason they were celebrating. Neil and Sara Logan's faith had been an integral part of all the preparations, from the extra baking their mother dropped off to elderly members of the congregation to curling up on the sofa together on Christmas Eve and listening to their father read the story of Jesus's birth from the book of Luke.

After living alone for so long, Jesse had looked forward to sharing the holiday with Marie, hoping that, as a couple, they could resurrect some of the family traditions he'd put aside while concentrating on the ranch.

But the first Christmas they'd spent together as husband and wife had been Jesse's wake-up call to the differences in their family backgrounds.

He had agreed to spend the holiday with Marie's parents because he knew how much she missed them. But in the Banner mansion, the house was decorated by a professional, who changed the "theme" every year. Marie's family didn't even trim the tree together, one of Jesse's favorite traditions. He could have dealt with that if it hadn't been for his new wife's complete indifference toward anything related to the true meaning of the day. She'd paid more attention to what her friends were wearing at the Christmas Eve service than the sermon.

They ended up arguing most of the drive back to High Plains, and Marie refused to speak to him for two days.

Merry Christmas.

Jesse averted his gaze. "No, Jesse doesn't know where the Christmas tree stand is."

At his abrupt response, Clay's eyebrows disappeared under the brim of his Stetson. Jesse didn't care. He wasn't ready to think about Christmas. Or pretend to look forward to Christmas. Not this year.

But apparently he was in the minority.

The whole town had pitched in over the past few months to rebuild the Old Town Hall. The mayor and Reverend Garrison hoped to have the project finished in time to commemorate Founders' Day with a special potluck and dance on Christmas Eve followed by a community celebration Christmas Day.

Jesse couldn't scrape up the desire to attend either one, and had turned down an invitation to speak at the gathering. Even though Mayor Lawson had reminded him that as a direct descendent of Will Logan, the man who had driven a stake in the ground near the High Plains River on Christmas day in 1858, people would expect him to attend.

Just the way Clay and Lori expected that he knew where to locate a tree stand on a moment's notice.

He cast an impatient look at his brother. "I don't know where it is because I haven't put up a tree for years. That's why I told Lori she shouldn't have gone to all this trouble. I usually spend Christmas at Maya's and I assume Lori will be going home."

The color drained out of Lori's face and Jesse took a step forward, concerned at the sudden change in her expression.

The oven timer in the kitchen pierced the sudden silence.

"Lori? Is something wrong?" Clay asked.

"No." She ducked her head and moved toward the door, refusing to meet their eyes. "I…need to check on something in the oven. Please excuse me."

She slipped out of the room and Clay aimed a scowl at Jesse. "What was that about?"

"I have no idea. You were standing here, too." Disturbed, Jesse listened to the sound of Lori's footsteps in the hall.

Clay's eyes flashed. "It's obvious you won the part of Scrooge this year, but I don't see why it should bother you that Lori wants to decorate the house or put up a tree."

"It isn't about that. It's about her taking time for herself," Jesse shot back, still shaken by the expression on Lori's face. "I know how demanding the triplets can be. Correct me if I'm wrong, but Lori deserves a day off."

"Since you're giving me permission, I will correct you." Clay met his gaze without flinching. "Because I thought having a day off meant doing what you want to."

"It does." Jesse frowned. Hadn't he just *said* that?

"So…" Clay drew out the word in a way that made Jesse's back teeth grind together. "Did it occur to you that maybe Lori was doing exactly what she wanted to do on her day off?"

"Extra work? Work she didn't need to do?" Jesse raked a hand through his hair. "You see how hard Lori pushes herself around here. If she doesn't slow down a little she's going to burn out and—"

Quit.

Jesse's mouth dried up, preventing the word from tumbling out. And hard on its heels rode another thought. He didn't *want* her to quit.

The speculative gleam that appeared in his brother's eyes made Jesse wonder if Clay hadn't filled in the blank.

"Listen, I don't claim to understand women—"

"That's a relief," Jesse muttered under his breath.

Clay ignored the comment. "All I'm saying is that what you consider extra work might not be work at all, from Lori's perspective. Think about it this way—we love the ranch even though the long hours and the constant demands would suck the life out of most people. To us, though, it gives back more than it takes. If I had to guess, I'd say that's the way Lori feels about taking care of you and the girls. You hired her to run the house but she's turning it back into a home."

That thought didn't terrify Jesse as much as the longing that unfurled inside a dormant chamber of his heart. He'd made the mistake of reaching for that dream once. Before he knew what it felt like to lose everything.

"I didn't hire her to do that. I don't *need* her to do that." If he said the words out loud, maybe it would make them true. His head knew it, but for some reason his heart stubbornly—and unexpectedly—refused to agree.

Clay blew out a sigh. "Maybe it's what *Lori* needs. Did you think about that? Nicki mentioned she was totally devoted to her job at the hospital—a job she gave up at a moment's notice to come here. Did you ever stop to ask yourself—or her—*why?*"

Without waiting for an answer, his brother stalked out of the room.

Chapter Nine

The sudden silence brought quiet but not peace.

Maybe it's what Lori needs.

Clay's words repeated in Jesse's head as he slumped down on the sofa and closed his eyes. Big mistake. His memory took advantage of the momentary lapse in his defenses to replay part of the conversation that had taken place in the attic.

The day he'd asked—with a touch of sarcasm that now made him wince—how she planned to find time to fix the rocking chair in between taking care of the triplets, cooking and bringing the house back to life. Lori had smiled and claimed she enjoyed doing all those things. That she found them relaxing.

But he hadn't listened. Hadn't wanted to believe it.

The image of her stricken face popped back in his mind and the next breath Jesse took actually *hurt*.

What had he said?

He lurched to his feet and got tangled in the handle of a canvas bag beside the sofa. Shaking it free, he accidentally released a ball of yarn. By the time Jesse chased it down, it had rolled under the coffee table and was about to disappear under the recliner.

"Gotcha." Jesse snagged it and started to wind up the loose strand. It led him back to a pair of knitting needles stuck in what looked to be a Christmas stocking still under construction. Jesse was no expert, but even he could see the level of skill it had taken to add a name above the prancing horse with a garland of holly around its neck.

Brooke.

On a hunch, he rummaged through the contents of the bag. Inside he found another one depicting a sweet-faced angel and bearing Sasha's name. There was also an enormous ball of sparkly white-and-gold yarn he guessed would soon take shape and become a stocking for Maddie.

Jesse felt the truth slap him upside the head.

He'd assumed the nanny he hired would carry out the list of duties posted on the refrigerator and take advantage of the free time in her schedule to live her own life. He hadn't expected one who not only gave a hundred percent of her time and energy to his daughters but also freely opened her heart to them.

Loved them.

The fog of pain Jesse had been living under lifted briefly, and he wondered why a woman as sweet and giving as Lori didn't have children of her own. Why didn't she have a husband who loved her to distraction? Who started and ended the day with her in his arms?

Jesse ruthlessly squelched the memory of the way Lori had fit perfectly in his arms.

Further proof that he needed to keep his distance.

If Jesse were honest with himself, he knew his

negative, knee-jerk response when he'd found Lori decorating the house for Christmas hadn't sprung so much from bittersweet memories of his parents as it had from fear. Fear that he was getting used to things he shouldn't. Dangerous things. The sound of Lori humming softly to his daughters as she got them ready for bed. Having someone to share a smile with over the triplets' antics. A light glowing in the kitchen window that drew him in like a weary traveler when he walked back to the house after finishing the evening chores.

A woman like Lori deserved a man whose heart hadn't been shredded with shrapnel from his past. A man who believed in love, not someone who knew all too well how fleeting that particular emotion could be.

Home for Christmas.

Lori's vision blurred as she took the steaming pan of corn bread out of the oven and sank against the counter.

It wasn't as if she could blame Jesse for assuming she had a home to go back to.

She'd found that most people didn't ask about her extended family. The few times her coworkers, when discussing their own holiday plans, had asked her when she was going home, Lori would simply explain that her parents had divorced years ago and now lived on opposite sides of the country. Leaving her in the middle.

To Lori, it seemed as if she'd been caught in the middle most of her life. Caught between two unhappy people who seemed to agree on only one thing—that once the "duty" of raising her ended, they would be free to live their own lives.

And they had.

She received the obligatory Christmas card from her mother every year and a phone call on her birthday, but the letters she'd sent to her father had been returned with no forwarding address.

The lack of warmth in the house where she'd grown up had fostered her childish dreams of a day when things would be different. She would create her own home—a place where everyone who stepped through the door would feel welcomed. Special. *Loved.*

But this isn't your home, she chided herself. *It's Jesse's. And if he doesn't want you to spend Christmas here, then you have to find somewhere else to go.*

If she talked to Reverend Garrison, Lori was sure he could connect her with an organization that needed volunteers to serve meals to shut-ins or the homeless on Christmas Day. There were hurting people everywhere who needed an encouraging word or someone to spend time with them. She could be that person. She'd done it for years.

So why didn't acknowledging that lift the weight pressing down on her heart?

Because this year you want things to be different. You want to be with the triplets on Christmas.

The truth filtered into her thoughts and just as Lori accepted it, another one followed close behind.

And you want to be with Jesse.

Lori pushed away from the counter, wrapping her arms around her middle as she took a distracted lap around the kitchen table and tried to push away the errant thought.

The light-headed, fizzy feeling that came over her whenever Jesse walked into the room simply meant that he was a handsome guy and she happened to be blessed with twenty-twenty vision.

Keeping a professional distance from a man who held everyone at arm's length should have been easy. If it weren't for the fact that over the past few days, when Jesse lowered his guard, she'd caught fascinating glimpses of a man who had the capacity to care deeply.

His more playful side came out when he interacted with the triplets, and his commitment to family was evident in the daily phone conversations he had with Maya. And although tension obviously existed between him and Clay, the thinly veiled regret she saw in Jesse's eyes whenever Clay was in the room told Lori he had a desire to make things right with his brother.

Jesse might act as if past experiences had stripped his heart bare, but Lori knew all it needed was some tending. There was still life there.

If only Jesse would recognize how much God loved him and wanted to fill the empty places that each loss had gouged out of his soul, he would have a great capacity to love.

And he would be easy to…love.

The thought that maybe, just maybe, she was already halfway there terrified her.

When Lori allowed herself to daydream about her future husband, she had always pictured a man who laughed easily and was never stingy with his affection. The opposite of her father. And even though she couldn't compare the two men, she knew that Jesse didn't trust easily.

It was the reason he'd fired five nannies before hiring her out of sheer desperation. The reason he rebuffed Clay's offers to take on more responsibility for the ranch.

The reason why getting close to him would be risky. And Lori was no risk taker. At least she hadn't been, until the day she set down her suitcase in Jesse Logan's driveway.

Her growing feelings for her employer were a complication she'd have to pray about. But at the moment, all she wanted to do was escape the cloud that had settled over her when he told Clay that she would want to spend Christmas at "home."

The irony? She'd been pretending that's where she was.

Lori blinked back the tears that stung the backs of her eyes. Jesse's reaction when he'd discovered her decorating the house couldn't have made it any clearer. He expected her to stick to the duties outlined on the index card.

As if Lori's feet had an agenda of their own, they carried her out of the kitchen and down the hall. She grabbed her jacket off the hook near the back door and slipped outside.

As busy as the triplets kept her during the day, Lori hadn't taken time to explore the ranch. Jesse had once suggested she use her free time to take a walk, so she decided to take him up on it.

As she came around the corner of the house, Jesse's dogs, Max and Jazz, bounded up to greet her. She'd seen the pair of Australian shepherds chasing each other around the barn on occasion, but hadn't had an opportunity to introduce herself properly.

"Are you going to give me a tour?" Lori reached down to ruffle one set of silky, speckled ears and then the other as the animals vied for her attention.

One of the dogs barked an affirmation and Lori chuckled, feeling her mood lift slightly. "Okay, then. Lead the way."

Maybe some fresh air would give her a fresh perspective. And while she prayed that Jesse would open his heart to God's love, maybe He would give her some wisdom so she would know what to do about her own.

* * *

She was gone.

Jesse looked in the kitchen and saw a pan of golden-brown corn bread cooling on the countertop and a kettle of chili simmering on the back burner, but there was no sign of Lori.

He bounded up the stairs but found the nursery empty, too. When he finally scraped up the courage to rap on her bedroom door, there was no response.

Where *was* she?

Panic scoured the lining of his stomach and Jesse hesitated in the hallway, unsure of where to look next. Or if he *should* look.

Clay had disappeared, too, so he couldn't ask him if knew where Lori might have gone. Not that Jesse would have risked getting another lecture from his younger brother. He wasn't used to Clay standing his ground and sharing his opinion about something.

Jesse walked to the nearest window and looked outside to see if Lori's car was still parked next to the barn. His relief at seeing the bright blue compact didn't completely dispel his growing concern over her disappearance.

He retraced his steps, forced to face the fact that Clay's insight into the reason behind Lori's actions may have been right.

He wasn't used to that, either.

In the past, Clay had operated under the "when the going gets tough, the tough take off" motto. The little brother Jesse had grown up with had been impulsive. Slow to think things through and quick to act.

That was part of the problem. Jesse was having a hard time relating to Clay because he was no longer a boy.

Growing up, the Circle L had formed the foundation of their relationship. When Clay stormed away and turned his back on the ranch that night, they'd lost their common ground.

"You're still brothers."

Something Maya had reminded him that afternoon. Jesse had never understood her unwavering belief that God would eventually help Clay find his way home and their family would be together again.

Now that they were, the rules had changed. *They'd* changed.

With tears in her eyes, his sister had pleaded with Jesse to start over with Clay. Jesse wasn't sure he could. In order to start over, didn't a person have to let go of the past? Or maybe, in his case, the past had to let go of *him*. Sometimes Jesse felt as if there were shackles around his feet, preventing him from moving freely. From moving forward.

Maya would say that's where God came in, but Jesse's faith had been so weakened, he no longer trusted it to hold him up, or to fill the empty pocket in his soul when someone else he cared about walked out of his life.

Right. That's why it's so much easier to push them away first.

Jesse blamed the sudden tightening in his chest on the unnatural quiet filling the house. He took the stairs two at a time and glanced into the living room. The logs in the fireplace had burned down to a glowing nest of coals, and even though the decorations gave the room a festive look, something was missing.

Or someone.

Someone to whom he owed an apology for whatever it was that he'd done that had snuffed the sparkle out of a pair of wide brown eyes.

If he could *find* the someone.

Jesse opened the front door and found his view obstructed by the monstrous evergreen that took up half the porch.

What had his lunatic brother been thinking? They'd be lucky if the thing would fit through the doorway.

Turning sideways, Jesse pushed through it, wincing as needles jabbed through the faded denim fabric of the shirt he wore. He accepted the pain as penance. In the two weeks since Lori had moved to the ranch, Jesse never had known her to be moody or withdrawn. She didn't even seem to need time away from the demands of taking care of three babies—and two bachelor ranchers.

Which made her unexpected disappearance even more troubling.

His gaze searched the outlying pastures in vain for a glimpse of copper, knowing Lori's hair would stand out against the hills like a cardinal on a snow-covered branch.

Maybe he should check the barn. Clay usually fed the horses around this time, and Lori could have ended up there. A tiny knot of envy uncurled in his chest at the thought of the easy, uncomplicated friendship Lori had struck up with his brother. As much time as she and Jesse spent caring for the triplets, Lori didn't seem as comfortable with him.

Why is that, do you suppose? Jesse silently countered in disgust. *Clay came home bearing gifts while you almost caused her to fall off the ladder.*

And speaking of gifts…

The glare Jesse leveled at the offending object should have caused it to spontaneously combust. Maya told him she would have the triplets home by seven, so now the sequoia—*spruce*—in the doorway was not only an obstruction but a safety hazard.

"Thanks, little brother," Jesse muttered under his breath. "You left me no choice."

Max and Jazz veered toward the barn, more than ready to rest after a long romp in the hills, while Lori continued up the driveway. While she'd set off to clear her head, she hadn't realized daylight had retreated, bowing to the shadows that crept in and filled the spaces between the buildings.

She quickened her pace, wondering if Maya had returned with the triplets. She hadn't planned to be gone so long.

Someone had left the porch light on, and as Lori got closer to the house, she noticed the Christmas tree was gone. No doubt Clay had already muscled it through the door. If Jesse hadn't put it through a wood chipper first.

Lori sighed. The fresh air had given her a fresh perspective. And the still, small voice inside told her that she owed Jesse an apology. She'd gotten so caught up in turning the house into a replica of the one in her dreams that she hadn't stopped to take his feelings into consideration.

When it came to Jesse, Lori was learning to look below the surface to the emotions simmering there. He may have sounded all calm and logical when he pointed out there was no reason for her to waste her time and energy on Christmas preparations, but the pain that honed an edge on the words revealed the truth.

She couldn't believe she hadn't thought of it before.

Five months ago, Jesse would have been looking forward to celebrating Christmas with his wife and their new babies, not being a widower and single father at the age of thirty-four. No wonder he'd looked as if she'd set fire to the living room instead of simply adding some decorations.

Show him that You haven't abandoned him, Lord. Remind him that the gift You gave at Christmas—Your Son—proves You love him...and help me put my own feelings aside and know that wherever I spend Christmas, You'll be with me.

Lori followed a trail of pine needles into the house and down the hall and paused in the living room doorway. Peeking into the room, she couldn't hold back a smile of delight.

The tree stood right where she'd imagined it. In the corner of the room, next to a whimsical, keyhole-shaped window fashioned from delicate pieces of stained glass.

The branches moved and Lori realized there was someone wedged between the tree and the wall.

"Clay, I didn't see you back there." Lori rushed over. "Thank you for putting the tree up! Did you need some..." *Help.*

The rest of the words died in her throat. Because it wasn't Jesse's brother who fought his way out from behind the branches.

Chapter Ten

Lori flushed under the weight of Jesse's gaze as it swept from her wind-kissed cheeks down to her feet, stopping to linger—with disapproval—on the cute pair of suede shoes he must not have considered official, regulation ranch wear.

"You found the tree stand." Lori made a desperate grab at one of the thoughts bouncing around in her head and managed to blurt out a complete sentence.

Instead of answering, Jesse stepped forward and Lori sucked in a breath as he reached out and caught her hands, folding them between his. The warmth of his skin melted a path down to her half-frozen toes.

"No gloves? No shoes?"

Lori glanced down at her feet. "I'm wearing shoes."

"Those aren't shoes." Jesse stalked toward the fireplace, shedding pine needles on the carpet as he tugged her along behind him. "Sit here for a few minutes and thaw out."

He didn't have to tell her twice. Lori sank onto the stone hearth, which felt better than her electric blanket, and closed her eyes blissfully.

When she opened them again, Jesse was still looking at her, the blue eyes unfathomable.

Lori swallowed hard. "Thank you for putting up the tree."

"It was blocking the door."

Of course it was. Lori forced a smile and rose to her feet. "I should put the ornaments on before Maya gets back with the triplets."

"You have—" Jesse glanced at the grandfather clock "—about twelve minutes and thirty seconds."

That would give her enough time to string the lights....

Except that someone already had.

She turned to stare at Jesse. "You put the lights on."

One of the broad shoulders lifted in a casual *so what if I did?* shrug.

"Were they...umm, blocking the door, too?" Lori ventured.

Jesse's bark of laughter surprised them both.

It also surprised Maya, who stood in the doorway, her eyes wide with disbelief. Disbelief that slowly changed to a speculative gleam, as her gaze shifted from her eldest brother to the new nanny.

Oh. No.

Lori had seen that expression before. Whenever one of her coworkers pulled her aside to tell her they had a cousin/brother/neighbor/friend who wanted to meet her.

"Unca Jesse." Layla's excited chirp momentarily distracted the adults, as she dashed into the room followed by a slender teenage girl with a self-conscious smile. "This is my new cousin Av'ry. She watches me and Tommy sometimes, but she likes your babies, too."

"So do I." Jesse smiled at Avery.

Lori let out a relieved breath as the little girl launched

herself at Jesse, who scooped her up in his arms. His niece giggled before planting a smacking kiss on Jesse's stubbly jaw. She drew back and shook a pudgy finger at him. "You're scratchy. Daddy's face doesn't feel like that."

Jesse arched a brow. "That's because your daddy talks to people all day and your uncle Jesse talks to horses."

Layla giggled again and Lori couldn't help but notice that Maya's eyes had misted over. She guessed the woman's emotional response came from hearing Layla call Greg Garrison "Daddy."

In a small town, everyone knew everyone else's business, so Lori had heard that Jesse's sister and Greg had recently exchanged wedding vows after a whirlwind courtship. The couple had started their marriage with a ready-made family in Maya's three-year-old daughter, Layla, but they were also in the process of adopting Tommy.

"Tommy talks to Charlie, too," Layla informed him.

At this, Jesse glanced at Maya. "You found Charlie?"

Maya's expression clouded. "Not yet. A few weeks ago someone called, claiming they saw a dog that matched Charlie's description down by the river, but Greg drove down there and didn't see any sign of him."

"Tommy says he'll be home for Christmas," Layla said. "He prays every night for Charlie. I heared him."

Jesse cleared his throat and gave his niece a playful tap on the nose. "Where are my babies, by the way? You promised to bring them back."

"In the car with Daddy. He said let him know when the toast is clear."

"Mmm." Jesse pretended to consider that bit of news. "Are you sure he didn't say *coast?*"

"Nope," Layla said decisively, as she struggled to get

down. "I'll get Tommy." The moment her feet touched the floor, she was off and running.

"Tommy is outside playing with Max and Jazz," Maya said softly. "He's been adjusting well to living with us but he really misses Charlie. Greg and I have talked about getting him a new puppy for Christmas, but maybe it's too soon. Tommy still believes Charlie is going to come back."

Before it occurred to Lori that it wasn't her place to offer advice, she shook her head. "You should wait."

Jesse tossed her an impatient look. "Maybe it is a good idea. Charlie isn't coming back."

"You don't know that." Lori didn't want to argue with him—could be grounds for being fired, after all—but she did think it might be too soon to replace Tommy's pet.

Jesse's lips tightened. "The dog has been missing since the tornado hit. I think it's better if you didn't let Tommy keep wishing for the impossible."

"But we don't know it's impossible," Maya said, her smooth forehead furrowing. "I think that's where Tommy's hope comes from. Every Sunday he asks me to read the praise corner in the church bulletin. After the tornado, Michael asked people to share stories of God's faithfulness, and each week, there isn't an empty spot on the page. This morning, a woman wrote that a family album with all her children's baby pictures was returned to her. Completely intact."

"It's nice to know that some people are finding the things they lost."

Sympathy flashed in Maya's eyes. "Jesse, you know we haven't given up hope about finding the ring."

"I have," Jesse said flatly.

Avery, Lori noticed, was listening to their exchange with wide-eyed interest.

A sudden commotion in the hall shut down the conversation and Clay wandered in, holding a bundled-to-the-chin and very wide-awake Sasha. "I hate to break up the party, but Greg and I could use some help with the baby brigade. And Maya, you should think about trading in that van for a coach bus."

Maya's lips curved into an affectionate smile as she looked at her niece. "We thought for sure the triplets would fall asleep on the way home, but they must have been afraid they were going to miss something."

Tommy appeared in the doorway, and the sadness in his eyes lifted a little as he caught sight of the tree.

"Are you going to decorate your tree tonight, Uncle Jesse? We made popcorn strings for the one we put up." His expression was earnest as he looked at his uncle. "The babies are too little to put the ornaments on, but we can help."

"We help," Layla echoed solemnly.

Lori couldn't look at Jesse. She was the one who'd inadvertently gotten him backed into a corner, so it was her responsibility to rescue him. Even though a tree-trimming party had always been high on the list of those childish dreams of hers that had been causing so much trouble lately.

She caught her lower lip between her teeth. There had to be a gentle way to turn down the children's heart-melting offer to help…if she could think of one.

"Lori?" Jesse's husky voice stirred up those mustangs again. She dared a look in his direction, and felt her heart buck at the sight of his rueful smile. "Do we have any…popcorn?"

Hope took wing inside of her. "I think we do."

"Great." He looked as if he actually meant it, but Lori knew better. The last thing he wanted to do was be reminded of his loss; but Tommy and Layla's feelings meant more than his own. It was one of the things she was beginning to love about him.

Like about him. One of the things she was beginning to *like* about him.

"Do you mind making some?"

"Yes. I mean *no*." Lori stumbled over the words as Jesse's smile widened into the captivating, take-no-prisoners smile that never failed to steal her next breath. "No, I don't mind. Not at all."

Tommy and Layla turned to their mother, who knew what was coming and held up both hands in surrender. "I suppose we can stay another hour to help Uncle Jesse and Lori, but that's it. Do you mind staying a little bit longer, Avery?"

"Great. I'll unwrap Sasha while Lori and Jesse collect the rest of their chicks." Clay toted his niece over to the sofa.

Lori ducked her head and made for the door before anyone noticed her freckles start to glow.

Their chicks?

Clay probably hadn't realized what he'd said. Or if he had, it was only a reference to the fact that she and Jesse cared for the babies together. It was a business relationship.

She knew that when Jesse hired her. But lately, all her good intentions had turned into wishes. She wanted more.

"Did you make this one?"

Jesse glanced at the cardboard candy cane dangling from Lori's fingers. "I plead the fifth."

"So, yes." Lori grinned. "Most people stick with red and white. I think it's very…creative."

"I think I wanted to use every color of glitter my Sunday school teacher put out on the table."

"Glitter?" Layla, who'd found a cache of tiny wooden carousel horses in the box of ornaments, perked up at the word.

Jesse cringed, imagining what would happen to a tube of glitter in the hands of a budding three-year-old Michelangelo.

"It's on the candy cane ornament your uncle made when he was little, sweetheart." A smile lurked in Lori's eyes as she held it up for Layla to see. "We were just admiring it."

Jesse couldn't help but notice the smile had been there all evening. It hadn't faded during the hundredth time she'd wound up the girls' infant swings, when Tommy accidentally dumped a bowl of popcorn over or when Layla draped gobs of tinsel on the spinning wheel when no one was looking.

Whatever had been bothering Lori, she must have left it outside in the hills, because she was obviously in her element.

Knowing that didn't let Jesse off the hook. He'd told Clay he didn't want Lori to suffer from burnout, but she seemed most content when surrounded by noise and activity. Which only reminded Jesse that he'd been out of line before.

"Pretty." Layla judged the candy cane "good" and went back to playing with the horses.

Lori leaned forward to hang it on the tree, but Jesse reached out and snagged her wrist.

"You aren't going to actually put that where people can see it?"

"Of course I am."

"No one is watching." Jesse lowered his voice. "Candy canes have been known to mysteriously disappear, you know. Never to be seen again."

Lori drew back, feigning alarm. "You wouldn't dare. This is part of your past."

"So?"

"So that means it belongs."

The woman was a walking Hallmark card. "It's proof that my mother never threw anything away."

Lori snorted. *Snorted.* "Trust me. In about four years, you'll have to build a separate storage unit to put every finger painting and Popsicle stick picture frame your daughters make in preschool."

Jesse opened his mouth to argue, and then snapped it shut as he tried to visualize tossing out anything of his daughters.

"Exactly." Lori laughed and every pulse point in Jesse's body leaped in response.

Self-preservation had him inching away from her. A challenge, considering that Layla and Tommy flanked them like bookends. Layla sat next to him, singing softly to her new friends, and Tommy stood beside Lori, trying to find out how many ornaments a single branch would hold.

Where were his sister and her husband, for crying out loud? Didn't they know Jesse had his own noisy brood to keep an eye on? Clay had joined in the festivities for a while, but then pulled a disappearing act, probably to make his nightly phone call to Nicki.

Jesse twisted around just in time to see Greg holding

a sprig of mistletoe above Maya's head. His sister blushed like a junior high kid at her first dance.

He was thrilled his little sister had fallen in love with a guy who actually deserved her, but couldn't prevent the wave of regret that crashed over him. Two years ago, when he met Marie, he thought he'd found what those daytime talk shows liked to refer to as a "soul mate." Now he suspected the term was nothing more than an advertising gimmick to sell more roses on Valentine's Day.

Did Lori like roses?

The thought breezed in uninvited and Jesse frowned. If she did, he didn't think she'd favor the perfect, elegant ones from a floral shop. No, given the enthusiasm Lori expressed for all the old stuff around the place, she'd probably prefer the wild, unkempt clusters of heirloom-pink roses that climbed the stone foundation of the house in late summer.

Alarms went off left and right at the sudden security breach inside his head.

"Mommy and Daddy are gonna kiss," Layla announced without looking up.

Avery, who sat on the sofa paging through a dog-eared copy of *The Gift of the Magi*, rolled her eyes.

"They do that." Tommy heaved a long-suffering sigh.

"'Cause they love each other," Layla said knowingly.

Tommy wrinkled his nose. "It's still gross—isn't it, Uncle Jesse?"

Jesse didn't want to think about kissing. Or *talk* about kissing. Especially not with Lori sitting so close. He glanced at her, careful not to let his gaze drift to the soft pink lips always on the verge of a smile. Her slender body was rigid, eyes staring straight ahead, and her lips—

yup, in spite of his noble intentions he'd looked anyway—were pressed together in a somber line.

It was obvious the topic was awkward for her, too.

Suddenly Lori's shoulders began to shake and she started to laugh.

And Jesse, in spite of himself, couldn't help but join in.

Maya's and Greg's heads snapped around, and Maya's blush deepened when she realized everyone's attention had shifted from the tree to her and her new husband.

Greg cleared his throat. "I think it's time the Garrisons went home," he announced. "Lori and Jesse have to put the babies to bed, and tomorrow is a school day for you two."

Tommy sighed again.

"I like school," Layla said primly.

"You would." Tommy crossed his arms and scowled.

Layla burst into tears.

"Whoa. Time-out, guys." Greg put his hands together like a referee. "We're all getting tired."

Without being scolded, prompted or cued, Tommy suddenly wrapped his arms around Layla and gave her a fierce hug. "Sorry."

Layla sniffed. "I forgive you."

Tommy fished inside his pocket and pulled out a mashed Tootsie Roll. "You can have this."

Squealing with delight, Layla pounced on the misshapen piece of candy and started to unwrap it. With a relieved smile, Maya herded the two children toward the door.

"We could all take a page from their book, couldn't we?" Greg murmured.

Jesse couldn't have agreed more. It was too bad all family conflicts didn't get resolved with an apology and a Tootsie Roll.

"I'll start the three *B*s," Lori murmured, as she rose to her feet. "You can see your sister and her family out."

Jesse noticed the candy cane still clutched in her hand. "You're going to hang that on the tree the minute my back is turned, aren't you?"

Lori flashed her thousand-watt smile. "Absolutely."

Chapter Eleven

"It's good to hear you laugh again." Maya whispered the words in Jesse's ear as she went up on her tiptoes to hug him goodbye.

"I laugh," Jesse muttered.

"Not often enough." The affection in Maya's eyes matched her tone. "She's amazing, Jess. A real answer to a prayer—I don't know how you managed without her."

Jesse didn't bother to pretend he didn't know who she was referring to. Sometimes it seemed as if Maya knew him better than he knew himself. "The girls seem to like her."

"The girls?" Maya repeated the words with a raised eyebrow.

"Yes. The girls." Jesse's eyes narrowed, daring his sister to continue down the path she was not so subtly hinting at.

He knew her, too.

"The house looks the way I remember it when we were growing up. All of Mom's old decorations." Maya smiled wistfully. "I'm glad she kept everything—and that you decided to put it up this year."

"It's not as if I had a choice."

Maya tilted her head. "She's good for you."

Here we go again, Jesse thought. "She's good for the *girls.*"

Maya didn't appear as if she'd heard him. "Tonight...I wished Mom and Dad were here. They would have loved watching Tommy and Layla have fun. And they would have spoiled the triplets rotten."

"Don't go there, Maya."

"Why not?" Her chin lifted. "I miss them, Jesse. Every day. Even though I can't see them anymore, I can still hear their voices. If we want to honor their memory, we have to remember what was important to them."

"The ranch." Jesse scraped an impatient hand through his hair. "Why do you think I'm still here?"

"Not the ranch." Maya's frustrated look judged him as dense as smoke from a brush fire. "Family."

She was referring to him and Clay again. He sighed. "You're pushing."

"Someone has to." Maya huffed the words, but Jesse could tell by the way her shoulders relaxed that she had decided it was time to back off. Until a teasing sparkle danced in her eyes. She peeked at him from under her lashes. "You are so stubborn, I'm surprised that Lori puts up with you."

He rolled his eyes. "And you are so transparent."

"Thank you." Maya beamed. "I take that as a compliment." She gave him another hug that threatened to cut off the flow of oxygen to his brain. "Thank you for putting up with us tonight."

"Thank Lori." Jesse nudged his sister toward the door, but Maya had to get the last word in.

"I did. Now make sure you do, too."

Jesse didn't bother to mention that not only did he owe Lori a thank-you, he owed her an apology, too.

Jesse met Lori at the bottom of the stairs.

"They're already asleep?"

"I'll have to give them their baths in the morning. I think watching their cousins decorate the tree completely wore them out."

Jesse wasn't surprised. It had worn *him* out. "Layla is just as precocious as her mother at that age. I remember Clay complaining to Mom once that Maya made his ears tired."

What made him think of that?

Jesse rocked back on his heels, unsettled by the thought. On the other hand, why should it come as a shock that an evening submersed in what his sister had warmly referred to as "making memories" had stirred up a few of his own?

For a little while, like a spectator swept into the middle of a holiday parade, Jesse had gotten caught up in the festive mood. He and Clay had even shared a knowing look at Tommy's excitement when Maya told him he could put the final touch on the Christmas tree—the gold star at the top.

Jesse wondered if witnessing a replay of that once-sacred Logan tradition had opened up a floodgate of memories for Clay, too.

Growing up, that particular honor had always fallen to Jesse. The year Clay turned seven, he questioned why

Jesse always got to put the star on top of the tree. Jesse had seen the deep disappointment on his brother's face and asked their parents if they could each put up a star.

"'Cause there is room for two," he'd told them.

Every Christmas after that, finding a tree that had room at the top for two stars had become a challenge that involved the whole family.

Unfortunately, Jesse's brain hadn't stopped with that memory. It hit fast-forward and took him to another place. The conversation that had taken place the night of his brother's senior prom. After he'd bailed Clay out of jail.

"Face it, Jesse. There isn't room on the ranch for both of us. You and I both know that Dad was grooming you to take over the Circle L. You don't need me."

"Don't be an idiot. This is your home. But if you're going to keep making decisions that ruin your life, at least go somewhere else so that Maya and I don't have to watch it happen."

Jesse hurled the words at his brother in anger, verbal fallout from the aftershocks of that late-night call from the police department. When he'd first heard the dispatcher's voice, he assumed the worst. He thought Clay was dead.

He hadn't expected his brother to leave the Circle L the next day. For good.

They'd always had a difficult time communicating, but the words they exchanged in the barn that night had become embedded in their relationship like a splinter. All these years, it festered below the surface, never quite healing. And Jesse didn't know how to remove it.

"I think Brooke is going to give Layla a run for her money in the precocious department."

Jesse's attention snapped back to Lori, as her soft voice

filtered through the dark shadows cast by the memory of that night.

"You are probably right," Jesse muttered. And multiplied times three, the thought of being so outnumbered was more than a little terrifying to a rookie dad.

"Don't look so worried. You'll do fine."

Jesse wasn't so sure. And the fact that Lori had accurately read his mind was somehow equally as terrifying.

In the short silence that filled the air, Lori skirted around him. But instead of going up the stairs, she headed in the direction of what used to be Jesse's normal, everyday living room, before its radical transformation into a life-size Christmas card.

"Just to warn you, that tree will tip over if you put another ornament on it." He found himself following her.

"I promise, no more decorating." With one finger, Lori drew an invisible X over her heart. "I thought I should do damage control before I collapse, too."

Jesse's eyes narrowed. She didn't *look* as if she were about to collapse. Strands of copper hair had escaped the elastic band of her neat ponytail, but the amber eyes hadn't lost their glow. He was relieved it had returned— even if he had to put up with the adverse side effects from the warmth of her smile. Rapid pulse. Shallow breathing. Light-headedness.

Lori went straight to the sofa and lifted one of the cushions, revealing a layer of popcorn as thick as insulation.

How had she known it was there?

Shaking his head, Jesse gathered up the rope of silver garland his niece had draped around her shoulders like a feather boa.

"It could have been worse, I suppose," Jesse said.

"Layla and Tommy could have insisted we break out the glitter and make more ornaments."

"Mmm." Lori knelt down, taking a sudden but keen interest in a string of lights drooping off the end of a branch.

"You volunteered to make ornaments with them, didn't you?"

The telltale flush of pink stealing into the porcelain cheeks answered his question.

"Next Sunday after church. On my day off," she added swiftly, as if anticipating his response.

Now he had guilt. And it tripped a switch on his memory. Once again, he saw Lori's stricken expression when he'd said…

What had he said?

Jesse still couldn't shake the nagging feeling there'd been more to her reaction than hurt feelings over his bungling attempt to spare her extra work.

"They'll like that." Jesse began to pick strands of tinsel off the spinning wheel, and they promptly attached themselves to his flannel shirt as if it were a magnetic field. "Isn't this stuff banned in the United States?"

"No, but it's definitely something the babies could get tangled in because it doesn't like to stay put," Lori said. "I didn't say anything because I didn't want to hurt Layla's feelings."

Because, Jesse's conscience cuffed him upside the head, *there are people who are sensitive about that sort of thing.*

"She'll notice it's gone the next time she visits," he pointed out.

"It won't be gone. It will be displayed in this special, star-shaped Christmas tinsel box."

The clear plastic container she presented for his inspection looked vaguely familiar.

"I think that was intended to hold half a pound of jelly beans." Green apple and cinnamon, if Jesse remembered right.

"Now it's going to hold tinsel." Lori held it out and Jesse dutifully transferred the clingy strands from his shirt into the container. "It will be safe from the triplets, but it'll have a place of honor when Layla visits."

"Where do you come up with this stuff?" Jesse wondered out loud, amazed by her creativity when it came to children. "Does it come naturally, or were your mom and dad famous parenting experts or something?"

Apparently, he was rustier at the whole teasing thing than he'd thought, because Lori's warm smile didn't surface. Instead, her eyes darkened with something that looked like...pain.

Something Jesse was shocked to see there, but recognized as easily as he recognized his own reflection in the mirror.

"No." Lori felt the container slide between her damp palms as she carried it to the mantel.

Jesse trailed behind her, collecting empty boxes and nesting them together along the way. "No to the first part, or no to the second?"

Lori had hoped a simple, straightforward answer would have been enough to satisfy Jesse's curiosity. She strove to keep her voice light. "No to both."

It wasn't as if she could tell him that there was nothing particularly unique or even instinctive about the way she related to children. Most of her ideas stemmed from wishes. The things she'd needed—wanted—*her* parents to do.

"Are you from a large family?"

The container wobbled. Lori didn't trust her hands to steady it, so she pushed them into the front pockets of her jeans. "I'm an only child."

An only child who didn't want to have this conversation.

She spotted a box of Christmas lights and made a break for it. Finding a vacant space on the floor—right next to the Christmas tree Jesse hadn't wanted—she drew out a knot of lights, hoping he'd be more than ready to retreat to his office where there wasn't a red velvet bow or ornament in sight.

He didn't.

Instead, he dropped into the chair beside her and picked up one end of the lights she'd started untangling. Connecting them by a single, dark green wire.

"Do your folks live around here?"

"No."

Jesse eased from the chair onto the floor beside her and she stiffened at his nearness. He reached into the box, tugging another set of lights free.

A long minute of silence stretched between them and Lori realized he was waiting for her to elaborate.

"Mother lives in New York." She held her breath, hoping he wouldn't ask the obvious: *What about your dad?*

"Do you usually spend Christmas with her? On the East Coast?"

Lori's fingers twisted together in her lap. "I picked up extra shifts at the hospital. People want to be with their families, and since I was single, I was the logical person to work over the holiday."

Jesse easily read between the lines. Lori had worked longer hours to help out her coworkers. But why hadn't she wanted to be with *her* family? Seeing how much she loved fussing over Christmas, wouldn't she want to go home?

The jolt that went through Jesse made him wonder if God hadn't just reached in and reconnected some faulty wiring in his brain. Before he could linger on the fact he'd just acknowledged God still might have a bead on Jesse Logan, the conversation they'd had earlier that afternoon rushed back in.

"I usually spend Christmas with Maya and I figured Lori would be going home."

Silently, Jesse lined up the casual statement against the wounded look in Lori's eyes that afternoon and came up with a match. Lori hadn't reacted to his implied criticism that she'd overstepped her bounds by decorating the house—she'd been hurt by his casual assumption that she had a place to spend Christmas.

Jesse felt the sting, as the truth sank into his thick skull. He'd assumed Lori was the way she was—all sunshine and smiles—because she'd been raised in a nurturing, loving family, protected from life's storms.

When he hired her, he hadn't thought that she'd given up her own home to move into his. She no longer had a living room to trim with colored lights, nor little bows nor a Christmas tree. Nor people to share those things.

His family had fractured after the death of their parents, but when Jesse thought about it, there were a lot of good memories to draw from. Loving parents. Laughter. Something he'd taken for granted.

Jesse drew in a slow breath, feeling his way through unfamiliar territory like a cowboy air-dropped into the middle of downtown Chicago. Now that he knew what he'd said, he wasn't sure how to make it better.

Five minutes later, he still wasn't sure. But he had to come up with something, because the lights were almost knot-free, and something in Lori's posture warned him that she was poised for flight.

"I was thinking about the dedication they're planning on Christmas Eve for the Old Town Hall," Jesse said casually. "My baby sister ordered me to go, but she's on the restoration committee. Between her responsibilities and her own family, she'll be pretty swamped. If you could stay with us over Christmas and help me with the girls, I'd pay you overtime."

Lori's next breath stalled in her chest, as hope bloomed there like an answer to a prayer she didn't even remember praying. But God must have seen it, tucked away in a corner of her heart.

"I could do that." Lori said. "But I won't accept any extra pay. It would be my gift."

Jesse was silent for so long that Lori wondered if he'd heard her. She decided God had given her an opportunity to follow the urging of that still, small voice she'd heard on her walk.

"Jesse? I'm… I owe you an apology." The words came out in a rush, keeping pace with the tempo of her racing pulse. "I didn't stop to think about how you might feel about Christmas this year. Without Marie. All the changes in your family. I should have talked to you first, instead of getting carried away with the decorations. It's your house."

She needed to keep reminding herself of that. Because it was starting to be so easy…too easy…to think of it as home.

Jesse's earlier silence had been disquieting enough, but this one stretched out so long Lori was tempted to grab her knitting bag and finish Sasha's Christmas stocking while she waited for his response.

"These are outdoor lights, you know."

Okay. Not the response she'd been expecting. But curiosity got the best of her. "How can you tell?"

"They're all clear bulbs. Mom used to wrap the porch rail outside with white lights."

Without closing her eyes, Lori could imagine how beautiful that would look.

"I could probably find some time to put them up. If you want me to."

Lori momentarily forgot it was safer to avoid looking directly into Jesse's blue eyes. But she wasn't sure she heard him right.

The regret she saw there squeezed the air from her lungs. But what did he have to feel sorry about?

"Really?" The word came out in a pitiful croak. "Thank you."

"And just for the record, you don't owe me an apology." Jesse's voice was low as he stared at the tree. "I owe you one. I didn't think about taking pictures of the girls with the Christmas tree in the background. Or how Layla and Tommy would enjoy the decorations when they came to visit. Sometimes I can't see…" He struggled to find the right words and finally gave up with a shrug. "Just do whatever you want to when it comes to Christmas preparations, and I promise to stay out of your way."

Lori knew what he'd been trying to say. Sometimes he couldn't see beyond his own pain.

Warmth spread through her, as Lori wondered if he even realized the significance of the moment. He wasn't fooling her. He'd picked up on her reluctance to talk about her family and guessed something wasn't right.

Jesse *had* seen beyond his own pain...when he'd caught a glimpse of *hers*.

Chapter Twelve

Jesse shifted his weight under the pickup truck, trying to dislodge the irritating object burrowing into his right shoulder blade.

By trial and error over the years, he'd taught himself how to fix the equipment that inevitably broke down. Clay had always been the one with a knack for coaxing engines back to life, but he wasn't available. For the past week, his brother divided his time between putting in a full day at the ranch and then driving into High Plains to act as foreman for the crew trying to get the Old Town Hall ready in time for the Christmas Eve celebration. The project was going on practically round the clock.

It crossed Jesse's mind that Clay was trying to earn the town's forgiveness for all the teenage pranks he'd pulled back in the day.

"You have to forgive him, Jesse. It's eating you alive."

Maya's words came back to him and the wrench slipped between Jesse's grease-stained fingers and clattered to the floor, missing his ear by an inch.

His sister was becoming more confrontational about the tension between him and Clay, and Jesse was getting tired of being her favorite target. When they'd talked on the phone the night before, she had the nerve to tell him that Clay was more than willing to make amends, but Jesse was the one who seemed reluctant to put the past aside.

All Jesse knew was that it *was* getting harder to hold the past up as a shield, protecting his defenses. Not when he no longer wanted to be Clay's boss. He wanted to be his brother. He wanted the easy camaraderie that he saw between Maya's husband, Greg, and his cousin, Reverend Garrison. He wanted to ease the burden of keeping track of the ranch's financial records onto Clay's shoulders, so he could spend more time with the girls in the evening.

And more time with Lori?

The unexpected voice in Jesse's head sent a chain reaction through his body that caused it to jerk. His shoulder bumped against the tire, which loosened a scab of rust above his head that rained down bits and pieces of metal like a broken piñata.

Great.

Lori was nowhere around and she was still a health hazard.

It was the reason he'd skipped supper and wandered through the outbuildings until he found an emergency that needed attention. Because he found it easier to deal with a fickle engine than fickle emotions.

Jesse wanted to spend time with her. And *wanting* to spend time with her had forced him to spend more time in the barn—so he *couldn't* spend more time with her.

No wonder the past few days had been pure torture.

If he timed things right, he could slip into the house at ten o'clock, when Lori was in her room for the night.

His fingers patted the dusty concrete floor to find the missing tool. The next thing he knew, someone's fingers brushed against his, soft as a whisper, and put the wrench in his hand.

Jesse didn't even have to turn his head an eighth of an inch to know who his mystery helper was. The subtle scent of wildflowers cut through the pungent smell of motor oil and grease, like the first spring breeze after a long winter.

His gaze slid over and collided with Lori's. She was on her knees next to the truck, peering at him with curious brown eyes. Her cheeks were pink from the cold, but her smile warmed him more than the space heater humming in the corner.

"Clay said you had an emergency before he left for town. I thought maybe it was one of the cows again."

Jesse had found the wrench—with a little help—but now he struggled to find his voice. "No cows this time. Just a broken driveshaft."

"I didn't know how long you'd be out here, so I brought you a cup of coffee and a sandwich."

Sure enough, Jesse caught a whiff of java. His nose twitched like Saber's when he tried to lure the horse into the round pen with a bucket of grain.

"Are the girls asleep?" He knew they were, or Lori would have never ventured outside.

"I have the baby monitor in my pocket." Lori's hand patted a bulge in her coat pocket. "The triplets all seemed a little tired today. Maybe they're having a growth spurt or starting to teethe. Anyway, I gave them their baths and put them to bed a little earlier tonight."

Jesse tried to ignore the guilt that the innocent comment stirred inside of him. He usually helped with the "three *B*s" every night, but he *had* warned Lori when he'd hired her that unexpected emergencies would come up. And even though the old pickup, rusting in the garage since the previous April, didn't quite constitute an emergency, it had provided an excuse for him to avoid having supper with Lori. Alone.

"You can leave it on the bench. I'll get to it in a minute." *As soon as you go back up to the house,* he thought. "Thank you," he added, because his mama had raised a gentleman.

Your daddy didn't raise a coward, either. But here you are, hiding under a truck.

Lori didn't budge. Jesse knew, if he moved his head a fraction of an inch to the right, he would see the delicate curve of her jaw.

He clenched his teeth and tried to focus on the task at hand, but his traitorous gaze drifted on its own accord to the glossy braid draped over Lori's shoulder, gleaming like polished mahogany against the green wool coat she wore.

Jesse heard a noise that sounded like the cap of a thermos being unscrewed, followed by the splash of liquid into a cup.

Don't look. Don't look. If you ignore her, she'll go away.

"Sasha sat up without any help from the bumper cushion this afternoon," Lori said, a hint of satisfaction creeping into her voice. "Her muscle tone is improving more every day."

Jesse blinked. Had she known he was concerned about that? Had he left the book on child development on the coffee table?

"I wish I'd seen it."

"You can," Lori said cheerfully. "I took a picture of her with my cell phone."

Jesse closed his eyes and groaned.

"Are you all right?"

"I'm fine. There's a…a rock or something digging into my shoulder." Immediately after he said the words, he realized his mistake. Lori was a nurse. Lori was a natural caregiver. Lori was already positioning her body to wriggle under the truck to help him….

"I think I will have that sandwich." Jesse shot out from underneath the pickup like a bronco released from a chute, then rolled to his feet. In the time it took to draw his next breath, Lori's efficient hands were brushing dirt off the back of his shirt.

He shied away. "It's fine. Thanks."

"Look." Lori flipped open her phone and, sure enough, there was a grainy image of his youngest, listing a little to the right but sitting up without assistance.

Jesse felt his throat tighten. The picture was another small affirmation that Sasha was going to be okay.

The day before, he and Lori had taken the girls to their appointment with Dr. Cole, and the pediatrician marveled at how far the triplets had come since their last checkup. She made a comment about all the TLC they must be receiving and gave Lori an approving look.

Right before they left, Dr. Cole pulled Jesse aside.

"Do you want my professional opinion, Jesse?" she murmured, while shuffling through the paperwork. "Don't let this one go."

That was the trouble, Jesse thought. The growing realization that he didn't *want* to let Lori go.

At the moment, however, his contrary nature wished she would. Unfortunately, she didn't seem to be in any hurry to leave him alone to enjoy his own, miserable company.

"This shed reminds me of the attic." Lori slid the phone into her coat pocket, retrieved the cup of coffee from the bench and handed it to him.

"I know. My family layered stuff in here like sediment." Jesse propped a hip against the hood of the truck. "Some of it dates back to the original homestead. Including the cobwebs."

Lori smiled and Jesse realized that had been his intent. To make her smile.

You are heading for trouble, buddy.

Jesse wanted to dive under the truck again. He hadn't been prepared for his heart and his head to wage a war over his growing feelings for Lori. He'd even come up with a list of reasons why he needed to keep a lid on them.

He was too old for her. Weighted down by too much baggage. What he had to offer wouldn't be enough, and eventually she'd find their relationship lacking. She'd find *him* lacking. And like Marie, she'd leave.

He wasn't convinced there was a whole lot of his heart left to offer someone. Especially someone like Lori.

"What is this? A metal detector?" Lori paused to inspect the high-tech gadget leaning up against the wall. "It looks new. Is it yours?"

"Yes," he admitted reluctantly.

"Do you look for things that belonged to your family when they settled the ranch?"

It would be easy to let her think that but for some reason, the truth popped out of Jesse's mouth. "I've been looking for Emmeline's diamond engagement ring. I'm sure you heard about it."

Lori tilted her head and frowned. "No. Should I have?"

"When Marie... The ring was on the kitchen table with her wedding band." No point in mentioning the note. "After the twister hit, I couldn't find it anywhere. People were finding things scattered all over the county, which was the reason Greg started the Lost and Found. Maya mentioned that Reverend Garrison made a special announcement about the ring one Sunday. He gave everyone a description and told people a little bit about its history."

"I worked a lot of weekends, so I must have missed it," Lori murmured. "That's what you and Maya were talking about the other night?"

Jesse shrugged. "She checks the Lost and Found every week. Hoping."

"But no one has found it yet."

Jesse didn't miss Lori's gentle emphasis on the *yet*. He wished he shared her and Maya's optimism. "At one point, it looked as if someone had turned it in, but the diamond was fake."

"I don't understand. Someone deliberately turned in a ring that looked like the one you'd lost?"

Jesse shifted uncomfortably. Even his cynical self had a hard time believing someone could be that coldhearted. But what was he supposed to think, when the evidence pointed in that direction?

"I'm not sure it was deliberate," he said slowly. "But the rings were similar in style. It's probably gone for good. What are the chances of finding a ring lost out there in the prairie grass?"

Knowing the chances were slim hadn't stopped him

from looking, though. When it came right down to it, Jesse felt responsible for that ring, and not only because it happened to be a family heirloom. Until he found it, it was another reminder that he'd lost something else he'd been responsible for. Something entrusted to his care.

Like Clay. And Marie.

"The diamond meant a lot to your family?" Lori ventured.

"It was passed down to the oldest son for generations. But if it's found, it would eventually go to Brooke."

Lori read between the lines. Jesse didn't think there would be any Logan sons. He didn't plan to marry again nor have any more children.

She wanted to wrap her arms around his lean waist... and shake the stuffing out of him.

Ever since the evening Jesse had inquired about her family, she sensed a subtle change in him. He'd been crankier than usual. He snapped at Clay. He could barely look her in the eye.

He'd also wrapped the porch rail in tiny white lights, hung a wreath on the lamppost and started to hum Christmas carols to the girls at bedtime.

Lori praised God for it all.

Jesse might not realize what was happening, but she didn't have to be a nurse to recognize the symptoms. Jesse was caught in a battle...with himself. And, if she wasn't mistaken, with God.

She prayed daily that God would not only break through the walls around his heart, but that He would give her wisdom to know how to protect hers.

Jesse wasn't the only one struggling. Lori had her own battle to fight.

No matter how often she reminded herself that Jesse was her employer, her heart didn't seem inclined to agree. It wasn't simply a matter of chemistry, either, although watching Jesse emerge from under the pickup—his dark hair tousled and a smudge of grease on his angular jaw— had given her heart a better workout than a half hour of aerobic exercise.

She thought she'd come to terms with her single status, content to trust God's timing when it came to finding love. The babies in the NICU had filled her arms and her heart.

Lori hadn't felt a void in her life. Until now.

She'd always taken for granted that the man God brought into her life would return her feelings. Not someone like Jesse, who had a deep capacity for love, but no longer trusted it.

His shuttered expression told her that he already regretted telling her about the missing heirloom.

Too late. Lori mentally squared her shoulders. Everyone else might back off when Jesse leveled that cool stare in their direction, but she was made of sterner stuff. Not to mention the fact that she had a very effective weapon to wield against the temptation to turn tail and run back up to the house.

I can do all things through Him who strengthens me.

In this case, the *all things* was reaching out to Jesse. Whether he wanted her to or not.

"I could help you look for the ring in the early mornings, before the triplets wake up," she offered.

There was a moment of absolute silence, and Jesse said, very carefully, it seemed to Lori, "I appreciate it, but there's no point now. The local weatherman predicted that the snowfall over the next few days is going to be significant." He tossed back the last of his coffee and pitched the empty sandwich bag into a bucket against the wall. "Thanks for bringing supper."

Lori recognized a hint when she heard one, but she was reluctant to leave Jesse alone, even if it was what he thought he wanted.

"You're welcome."

Jesse's eyes narrowed. "You look half-frozen."

"I'm fine." She forced a smile as her numb toes curled in denial.

"Your cheeks are red."

Lori put the blame on Jesse, not the temperature. She blushed whenever those stunning blue eyes turned in her direction. Why couldn't she have been a brunette instead of a redhead with pale skin that acted like a barometer for her emotions?

She resisted the urge to press her mittens against her face. "Are you coming back up to the house now?"

"Not yet." Jesse knelt down and rummaged around in the toolbox beside the truck. "Not for a long time. Could be hours yet. You know how tricky driveshafts are."

Lori didn't, but she wasn't ready to give up. Call her crazy, but she enjoyed Jesse's company—when he wasn't trying so hard to be disagreeable. The more time they spent together, the more she realized his gruffness was an effective way of keeping people at arm's length.

Lori might have been put off, too, if it hadn't been for the triplets. Jesse's love for his daughters peeled back the layers of his heart and revealed his true character.

The trip to the pediatrician the day before would have tested anyone's patience, but Jesse had responded to every unexpected situation—including a leaky diaper—

with a gentle confidence that increased her respect for him even more.

Made her want to be with him even more.

Aware of Jesse watching her, Lori pretended to be interested in the collection of rusty horseshoes hanging on the wall. A movement in the shadows caught her attention, and she peered into the darkness, startled at the sight of a pair of gleaming yellow eyes peering back at her. Her pulse evened out when she realized it wasn't an oversize rat but a harmless calico cat curled up on an old couch.

She reached out a hand and rubbed her knuckles under the cat's chin. "I've never seen him before."

"He keeps to himself most of the time."

Something in common with his owner, Lori thought wryly.

"What's his name?"

Jesse hesitated a fraction of a second. "Cat."

Lori chuckled. "That's the best you could do?"

"It's as good as any." Jesse shrugged. "Cats don't answer to a name, anyway. They answer when they feel like it."

She smiled when the animal's eyes drifted closed. "Well, he must be pretty spoiled to have his own velvet couch to sleep on."

"Velvet couch? I don't think anyone stored furniture out here." Jesse stalked over to investigate and dismissed her claim with a shake of his head. "This isn't a couch. It's an old cutter."

"Cutter?"

"A sleigh." He rearranged the clutter until the sleigh was completely visible. "See the runners?"

Entranced by the sight of the old-fashioned sleigh, Lori crowded closer. "You didn't know it was here?"

Jesse rubbed his jaw. "I forgot about it, to tell you the truth."

Lori clucked her tongue. "I can't believe that."

"Believe it." Jesse kicked one of the runners with the toe of his boot. "This isn't exactly a practical vehicle to have on a ranch—especially in the Flint Hills."

"It might not be practical, but it's beautiful." Lori's fingers smoothed the dusty velvet cover. "Did you ever use it?"

"Me? No." He looked disturbed by the question.

"Why not?"

"It's kind of a...*froufrou* thing, isn't it?"

"Froufrou?" Lori repeated. "Oh, I get it. There's no saddle, and you wouldn't be able to win the race against the dogs when you come back to the barn for lunch."

Jesse stared at her and Lori winced. Maybe she shouldn't have mentioned that. It sounded as if she spied on him. And she didn't. It's just that he looked good on a horse. Really good.

The corner of Jesse's lips twitched and Lori swallowed hard. No way. He couldn't have known what she was thinking.

She forced her stubborn vocal chords to do their job. "Someone must have thought it was fun, or it wouldn't be here."

"I can't imagine hitching up one of the horses to this contraption."

"You may have to someday. When the girls are a few years older, you might want to take each of them for a ride around the yard. Make it an annual tradition at Christmas."

"Wait a second." Jesse's eyes narrowed suspiciously. "This sounds like the 'making memories' stuff that my sister is always preaching about."

"It doesn't matter what you call it," Lori said patiently. "It boils down to *time*. And attention. Girls need to know they're special. Every time one of them tries to get your attention, she's asking you if she's important. If she's worth noticing. It will be easier to understand and accept God's love if they have a father who shows it first."

She hadn't meant to sound so passionate, but instead of becoming angry or defensive, Jesse regarded her thoughtfully. "Did yours?"

Lori's breath hitched in her throat. "I…" She moistened her chapped lips. "I… You have work to do, and I should probably check on the girls."

"Lori—" Jesse's voice reached her at the door, but she pretended not to hear.

It occurred to Lori as she hurried up the driveway that she was guilty of the very thing that frustrated her about Jesse.

She'd run away.

Chapter Thirteen

It took every ounce of Jesse's self-control not to follow Lori up to the house.

You wanted your own company, he reminded himself disgustedly.

Why would Lori want to spend time with him anyway?

He was rusty at small talk and his heart had disconnected from his brain a long time ago, giving him a distinct disadvantage when it came to understanding certain things. Like why a hundred-year-old sleigh could be an effective tool for connecting with the women in his life.

He tossed the wrench back in the toolbox and closed his eyes to block out the memory of Lori's expression when he'd asked her about her father.

It didn't work.

Once again, he'd caught a flash of sorrow in her eyes and it made him curious. No, it made him want to comfort her.

Another feeling he wasn't prepared for.

"It's none of my business," he told Cat. "That's one of the reasons we're out here in the cold garage and she's up at the house."

Not to mention it was safer that way. *He* was safer that way.

Cat obviously disagreed, because he yawned and jumped down from the sleigh before disappearing into the shadows. Leaving Jesse to carry out his self-imposed exile alone.

For the next hour, Jesse fixed the driveshaft, swept up the floor and straightened the horseshoes on the wall. At ten o'clock, he closed the garage and headed up the driveway, relieved to see the house was dark except for the light Lori always left on in the kitchen.

The smell of gingerbread greeted him at the door.

Lori had been baking up a storm over the past few days, much to Clay's delight. She'd copied their grand-mother's fudge recipe, frosted enough sugar cookies to feed an army and always kept water simmering on the stove for hot chocolate when he and Clay came inside.

When Jesse gave Lori the green light to continue her Christmas preparations, she proceeded to turn the entire house into a wonderland for the senses.

Jesse's lips curved. If he were honest with himself, he'd had more fun watching *her* than he had watching the house's gradual transformation over the past few days.

He shed his coat and boots in the laundry room and paused outside the kitchen door, positive she'd gone upstairs for the night. Maybe it wouldn't hurt to see what she'd made....

"Gingerbread with whipped cream."

Jesse whirled around and found Lori behind him. For some inexplicable reason, the room always seemed brighter when she was in it.

"I thought you'd be upstairs." *Or I'd still be in the garage.*

"Sasha woke up for a few minutes." Lori smiled. "Are you hungry?"

"No." Jesse hoped his stomach wouldn't growl and make a liar out of him. "I have some work to do on the computer."

For a split second, disappointment clouded her eyes. "I understand."

No, you don't, Jesse wanted to say. But he wasn't about to try to explain that every minute he spent in her company made him want to spend another…and another.

Jesse thought his heart had shut down after Marie's death, but whenever Lori was near, he felt as if it were slowly coming back to life.

He couldn't explain that, either. Not when he didn't understand it himself.

Lori sat up in bed, wide-awake. It felt as if she'd been asleep for hours but a glance at the clock told her it was just after midnight.

The faint whimper from the nursery wasn't an unusual sound to hear during the night, but this one, followed by a rasping cough, had Lori reaching for her robe.

Guided by the glow from the night-light, she padded quietly over to Sasha's crib. Even before Lori saw the baby crowded into a corner, she sensed something was wrong.

As she bent over the rail, Sasha let out another low, pitiful cry and rubbed her face fitfully back and forth on the mattress.

"Hey, peanut," Lori whispered, using one of Jesse's favorite pet names for his youngest daughter. "What's the matter?"

Sasha reacted to the sound of her voice with a mournful whimper. Lori picked up the baby and her heart dropped as she felt the heat radiating through Sasha's terry cloth sleeper.

A hundred-degree temperature—maybe higher, she guessed.

Lori carried Sasha to the changing table and pulled open one of the drawers, glad she'd taken the time to stock it with basics, like a brand-new thermometer.

As she took the baby's temperature, Brooke woke up and sneezed several times in a row, which jump-started a confused, unhappy cry.

"I'll be there in a minute," Lori promised, in a soothing voice. "Now, let's see what we've got here." She bit her lip as the digital readout appeared on the tiny screen. "One hundred and one. Oh, sweetheart. I'm sorry."

Sasha tried to work up a smile, but another cough twisted her body. Lori picked her up, cuddling her close as she went to check on Brooke.

One look at the baby's fever-bright eyes and rosy cheeks and she knew Brooke was running a temperature at least as high as her sister's.

Panic scrambled for a foothold and Lori took a deep breath, knowing her nurse's training would only go so far. Her faith would carry her further.

She closed her eyes.

Lord, please protect the girls. You know how small and vulnerable they are. And help me have the energy and strength to care for them—

"Lori? Is everything all right?" Jesse's husky voice coming from the doorway interrupted her prayer.

She hated to tell him the truth. "Sasha and Brooke aren't feeling well."

The light flipped on and Lori saw Jesse bearing down

on her, clad in a pair of black sweatpants and tugging a loose-fitting T-shirt over his head. Judging from his tousled hair and blurry eyes, he must have been sound asleep, until Sasha's cries woke him up, too.

Sasha kicked her legs weakly and made a valiant attempt to smile at her daddy—something that wrenched Lori's heart.

"What can I do?" Jesse looked wide-awake now.

"You can hold Sasha for a few minutes while I take a look at Brooke." Lori gently transferred the baby into Jesse's arms and saw the flare of panic in his eyes.

"She's burning up."

"She has a hundred and one temp." Lori deliberately kept her voice even to keep Jesse calm.

It didn't work.

"You already took it? Is that high? Is she teething? Does she have a cold? An ear infection?"

"I'm not sure yet." Lori picked up Brooke and walked back to the changing table. The baby's soft, miserable sniffle was somehow worse than the loud protests they'd grown accustomed to hearing from the eldest triplet. "Brooke feels a little warm, so we'll check her temp, too."

"They have the same thing?"

"It looks that way." Lori kept one eye on the rise and fall of Brooke's chest as she changed the baby's diaper. Other than the congestion in their noses, both the girls' breathing sounded fairly normal. But after Jesse left, she planned to listen to their lungs with the stethoscope tucked away in her dresser.

"Maddie?" Jesse's gaze shifted to the only occupied crib in the room.

"She seems to be fine. Sound asleep through all the commotion."

"She takes after Clay." Jesse's growl sounded more affectionate than gruff for a change. "You could have lit a stick of dynamite by his head when we were kids and he would have slept through it."

Lori held up the thermometer and Jesse pressed closer, waiting for the verdict.

"One hundred and one."

"Is that high?"

"It's elevated, but not dangerously so for a child. I'll give her and Sasha a dose of medicine to bring down the fever and make them feel more comfortable."

"And then what?"

"You go back to bed and I'll take it from here."

Jesse's eyes narrowed. "You've got to be kidding."

"I'm a nurse." Lori struggled to keep her voice light so he wouldn't worry. "It's not the first time I've stayed awake all night with a fussy baby in my arms."

"But this time you've got *two* babies and *one* set of arms," Jesse pointed out. "I'm staying. I wouldn't be able to sleep anyway. Not knowing…"

His voice trailed off and the lost look in those indigo eyes made Lori want to comfort *him*. It was frightening enough for a parent when a normally healthy baby contracted a cold, but much harder to deal with when the baby's health had been fragile from birth.

Lori pushed aside her own concerns about the girls for the moment and tried to think of a way to ease his mind. She flashed a mischievous smile. "I won't turn down the help. Do you want the rocking chair or would you rather *boggle?*"

Jesse stiffened and Lori hoped he would understand that she wasn't making light of the situation but trying to ease the tension.

His lips curved into a smile. "You and Sasha take the rocking chair. Brooke and I will boggle."

"Deal."

The next few hours passed by in a blur. Both Brooke and Sasha dozed off for short periods of time and then woke up with distressed cries, as another coughing jag or sneeze disrupted their sleep.

Brooke's fever went down significantly as the night wore on, but Sasha's stubbornly inched toward one hundred and two. Every time the baby looked up at her with confusion in those wide blue eyes, it tore at Lori's heart.

She checked temperatures every hour and tried to coax both Brooke and Sasha to drink some fluids. Jesse had more success at getting Brooke to take a bottle than Lori did with Sasha, so they traded babies several times.

In spite of the worry banked in Jesse's eyes, he was a huge help. She didn't know how she would have managed without him.

Fatigue dragged at Lori's limbs and tugged at her eyelids as she rocked Sasha.

"What else can we do?" Jesse paused as he and Brooke took another lap around the room, his expression dark with worry and helplessness at his inability to ease his daughters' suffering.

"Their ears don't look infected, so if it's a virus, as I suspect, it has to run its course. I'll call Dr. Cole in the morning, but there isn't a lot we can do but try to keep them comfortable."

"It doesn't seem like enough."

A pitiful chirp came from Maddie's crib and they exchanged grim looks. Jesse was at his daughter's side in a moment and his ragged exhale warned Lori the night was about to get longer.

"Should we recruit Clay?" Lori offered the tentative suggestion, not sure how Jesse would react to the idea of asking his brother for help.

"He isn't here. He called a little bit after ten and said he planned to spend the night at Maya's. They're so close to finishing the Old Town Hall that he wanted to work as long as possible. I guess it's just the two of us."

The two of us. Maybe she was getting punchy from lack of sleep, but Lori liked the sound of that.

"I'll take her temperature." She put Sasha down in her crib and gave the baby's toes an affectionate tweak. "Don't worry, I won't forget about you."

As it turned out, Maddie seemed to have the mildest symptoms of the three, but now that she was awake, she didn't want to miss out on any of the attention.

Jesse ended up holding both babies while Lori retrieved Sasha from the crib and continued to rock her. A few minutes later, she heard Jesse's footsteps pause close by.

"Lori? Are you asleep?"

Lori's eyes snapped open. "Of course not!"

"Your eyes were closed."

"I was praying." She was too tired not to tell the truth.

Chapter Fourteen

He should have known.

Over the past few hours, his own desire to pray for his daughters had been overwhelming, but as soon as the words formed in Jesse's heart, his head questioned whether it would do any good.

He remembered the times when he'd been sick, and his mother would sit on the side of the bed, fluffing pillows and doling out cough syrup. Like Lori, her whispered prayers for comfort and healing had been a natural part of her nursing regime.

After his parents' death and Clay's departure, Jesse hadn't found much comfort or healing in prayer.

Maybe because you stopped talking to God?

Jesse couldn't deny the truth.

The night of the tree trimming party, Maya had told him their parents would have wanted them to remember the things they had valued the most. Faith. Family. Things Jesse had somehow forgotten when he focused his attention on keeping the Circle L as successful as it had been when his father was alive.

Lori's honesty struck a chord in Jesse, and he found himself responding the same way. She seemed to have a way of bypassing his defenses and getting right through to his heart.

"I used to believe that God listens. Now I'm not so sure." What Jesse hadn't realized until now was how much he wanted to believe it. "I'm not sure about anything anymore."

Lori didn't appear to be shocked by the disclosure. "He does listen. Because He loves us."

"I wish I could be sure about that, too." There. He said it. Jesse waited for the disapproval, or worse, disappointment, he knew he'd see in Lori's eyes for voicing those kinds of thoughts out loud.

"You can be."

"Really." Jesse would have raised an eyebrow but his face was too tired to do anything more than twitch. She sounded so certain. Maybe because nothing had ever happened that caused her to doubt it, he reminded himself cynically.

"You believe in Him, don't you?"

The simple question broadsided Jesse and his chin jerked in affirmation before he thought it through. "Yes."

Lori didn't look shocked by that, either. Although Jesse knew she would have seen precious few signs of his faith over the past few weeks.

His lips twisted. Who was he kidding? More like the past few years.

Lori's eyes met his and Jesse expected to see sympathy. What he saw instead was acceptance. And then determination.

"When I was a freshman in college, Lynnette, one of the girls on my floor, led me to Christ," she said. "Lynn invited me home to spend Christmas with her family, and she could tell I was still struggling with something that happened in my…past." Lori looked down at Sasha, who lay quietly in her arms, as if reluctant to disturb the outpour of memories.

"I was questioning God. Wondering why He'd allowed it to happen. She said it was normal to have questions, but there was one I *never* had to ask. Does God love me? She said He answered that question at the manger, when He sent His son to earth. I realized that if I believe God loves me, I can trust Him to walk with me—or carry me—through the difficult things that happen."

For the past five months Jesse had received—and most of the time simply endured—dozens of well-meaning platitudes. Somehow, Lori's simple reminder of God's love began to erode the mortar of grief in the walls around his heart.

"Would you like to hear the verse she encouraged me to memorize?" Lori asked.

Jesse almost smiled. "Do I have a choice?"

A hint of a sparkle shimmered in her eyes. "Not unless you want to take the babies' temperatures next time."

Jesse winced. "Tell me the verse."

"It's from the book of Lamentations. *'Yet this I call to mind and therefore I have hope. Because of the Lord's great love we are not consumed, for His compassions never fail. They are new every morning,'*" she recited softly.

Unfortunately, Jesse knew what it felt like to be consumed.

What he didn't know was how to struggle free from the past.

"Calling it to mind," Lori said softly, as if she'd read his thoughts. Again. "It means *choosing* to remember that God loves us. No matter what happens. And we cling to that and go on from there, trusting that His great love means we are never without hope. He'll never leave us."

The note of sincerity in Lori's voice made it sound as if she spoke from experience and wasn't repeating something she'd read on the back of the church bulletin.

"What?" Lori shifted under the intensity of his gaze.

"That's why you love Christmas, isn't it?"

"Love Christmas?" Lori looked bewildered at the sudden turn in the conversation.

"I thought you just liked to fuss over the decorations and the making memories stuff," Jesse mused. "But it's because of what your friend, Lynnette, said, isn't it? About the proof of God's love being settled at the manger."

"Weren't we talking about you?" Lori's cheeks turned an appealing shade of pink as she averted her eyes.

Jesse was a little stunned to discover that he wanted her to trust him. Her abrupt departure the night before told him his question about her father had touched a nerve. She generously gave to others but seemed to draw back when it came to allowing others to reach out to *her*. He wanted to know her. Scary stuff for a man who'd decided that he wasn't going to let anyone get close. But he hadn't anticipated he would want to get closer to *her*.

Brooke let out an unhappy squawk, granting Jesse a brief reprieve from another unexpected revelation. He took her for another lap around the room to give his brain a chance to catch up with his heart. He'd never opened up about his faith—or lack thereof—after Marie died. Not even to Maya or Reverend Garrison.

"Jesse?" Lori called to him softly, as he finished lap number three. "Look who finally fell asleep."

"Sasha." Relief surged through Jesse as he looked down and saw that his daughter's eyes were closed, the fringe of dark lashes fanned out on pudgy, tear-stained cheeks.

"And Brooke." Lori's weary smile bloomed as her gaze lingered on the baby in his arms.

Jesse had been so lost in thought, he hadn't realized Brooke had fallen asleep. He laid his cheek against hers and the satiny skin felt cooler to the touch.

Thank You, Lord.

For once, Jesse didn't suppress his natural inclination to talk to God. For the first time in a long time, it felt…right.

"I'm going to put Sasha back in her crib now and see if she'll sleep for a while. Before it's time…" Lori stifled a yawn. "To get up."

Jesse noticed the pale streaks of silver lightening the horizon and grimaced. "I think it *is* time to get up."

"Then I'll hook up an IV to the coffeepot."

He choked back a laugh, a little amazed at how quickly—and easily—it had surfaced.

Lori gave him a stern look and put a finger to her lips, careful not to wake up Sasha as she carried her across the room.

Jesse followed suit and put Brooke down, too. He and Lori turned away from the cribs at the same time and ended up face-to-face.

She was beautiful. Even with lavender shadows under her eyes and unkempt wisps of hair framing her weary features.

Without thinking, Jesse reached out and lifted a loose strand of copper hair, tucking it behind her ear. It felt like satin between his fingers, just like he knew it would.

Lori's eyes widened as Jesse's fingertips traced a whisper-light path down the side of her neck.

"Thank you," he murmured. "For…everything."

Lori nodded, and the fact that she didn't move away made it that much harder not to take her in his arms. The only thing that stopped him was knowing that if he did, he wouldn't want to let her go.

"Hey, what's going on?" Clay's cheerful baritone boomed from the doorway. "Did my nieces decide to get up extra early to help with the chores this morning?"

His brother's timing, Jesse thought grimly, could have been a little better. And yet again, maybe he'd appeared in the nick of time.

Lori watched Jesse nudge his brother into the hall-way, and she forced her sluggish feet to follow, still a little dazed by the expression she'd seen in Jesse's eyes.

He'd wanted to kiss her.

Confusion churned in her stomach. Lori had assumed her feelings for Jesse were one-sided. Given her limited experience when it came to relationships, she didn't know if he was aware of—let alone felt—the tiny electrical charges that pulsed between them if they accidentally touched while giving the triplets their baths or traded babies during the bedtime routine.

Only, this time Jesse's touch hadn't been accidental.

She'd seen the conflict in his eyes when he looked down at her. Or maybe she'd seen her own emotions reflected there.

"The girls were up most of the night with high fevers," Jesse explained to Clay in a terse whisper, as he pulled the door closed behind them. "They just fell asleep a few minutes ago."

Clay's smile faded, replaced by concern as he looked at Lori. "Are they feeling better now?"

"Their temps seem to be going down," she replied.

"There must be something going around. Nicki mentioned that Kasey seemed lethargic yesterday. She even left work early to put her down for a nap in her own bed."

"Mmm. A nap."

Jesse's sharp look told Lori that she'd said the words out loud.

"Why don't you go back to bed for a few hours," he suggested. "I can hold down the fort until they wake up."

Clay slanted a skeptical look at his brother. "You look dead on your feet, too. Maybe *I* should be the one who holds down the fort. Since I wasn't here to rock a baby to sleep, the least I can do is make breakfast."

"Sounds good to me."

Clay looked shocked at his brother's easy acceptance of the offer.

Lori's heart lightened. Over the past few days, Clay had given Jesse's bad mood a wide berth, and Lori hoped the change she was witnessing in Jesse now was continued proof of God's faithfulness.

Jesse was His child and He wasn't going to let him go.

Once again, she was amazed at how the Lord brought good things out of difficult situations. Walking the floor with the triplets all night had opened up the door to a conversation she and Jesse might never have had under ordinary circumstances. It also had given her another glimpse into Jesse's heart. She no longer saw a man who'd rejected his faith, she saw a man struggling to rebuild his life on the foundation of that faith, but not sure how to go about it. What he didn't seem to realize was that rebuilding took time and patience. And forgiveness.

"I'll get started. Scrambled eggs and sausage? Pancakes? Fried potatoes?"

"Yes," Lori said instantly. "And coffee."

Clay chuckled but Jesse didn't join in. In fact, now he seemed to be avoiding her eyes. She was relieved when he accompanied his brother to the kitchen, sharing the details of the long night they'd had with the triplets on the way down the stairs.

She hoped there was one detail he *wouldn't* share.

Nothing happened, Lori reminded herself, ignoring the pulse that still jumped in the hollow at the base of her throat. The very spot his hand had lingered at after he'd tucked her hair behind her ear.

Jesse had simply…thanked her.

But for what? For helping with the babies? For encouraging him to go back to the core of his faith? For reminding him that God loved him?

The questions spun confusing circles in her brain, as Lori retreated to her room for a quick shower. The warm water revived her enough that she was able to ignore the comfortable bed as she pulled on a pair of jeans and a sweater.

Guided to the kitchen by the sizzle of bacon frying, Lori found Jesse already sitting at the kitchen table, his lean fingers linked around a mug of freshly brewed coffee.

Clay smiled and pointed the spatula at an empty chair across the table from Jesse. "Sit. Recover."

"He took over," Jesse murmured.

"Only because you're tired. I figured it was only fair that I take a turn at being the boss." Clay winked at her as he set a cup of coffee in front of her. "You should have called Maya's and let me know about the triplets. I would have come home right away."

Jesse was silent for a moment. "I didn't think…"

"I would," Clay finished the sentence. "Sometimes all you have to do is ask, Jess. That's what family is for."

Lori tensed, waiting for a terse comeback, but Jesse shot his brother a rueful look. "It's beginning to…sink in."

"What's beginning to sink in?" Maya breezed into the kitchen with Greg close behind. "That you aren't a superhero?"

Lori's lips twitched and Jesse leveled a *don't say one word about the guy in the pink tasseled blanket* look.

"It's too early in the morning for company," he complained, sinking a little lower in the chair. "Especially when a guy's been up all night."

"Company?" Maya rolled her eyes. "We're not company. We're here to take a shift." Her lively gaze swung from her brother to Lori. "You were right, Clay. They do look terrible."

Jesse scowled at Clay as the reason for Maya and Greg's impromptu visit became clear. "I thought you outgrew tattling."

Clay loaded a stack of buttermilk pancakes onto a platter and brought it to the table. "It's only tattling when you're under the age of ten. After that, it falls under the category of sharing information."

Maya pulled out a chair and sat down next to Lori. Jesse's sister had the radiant look of someone who'd actually gotten a good night's sleep.

"Don't you two have jobs?" Jesse asked as she reached for his cup of coffee.

"I have a very understanding boss." Maya gave her husband a saucy wink.

"A boss who can take the day off when there's a family emergency," Greg added.

"Don't worry about a thing," Maya said blithely. "Grab a long nap, both of you, or you'll never make it through the day, let alone another night, if they're up again." After taking a sip of Jesse's coffee, she plucked the fork out of Jesse's hand and stabbed one of the sausages on his plate. "I'll clean up in here."

"I'll bet you will." Jesse accepted another fork from Clay.

Lori's head started to swim. Whether it was from sleep deprivation or an attempt to follow the conversation, she wasn't sure.

"I don't think I'll be able to fall asleep," she offered tentatively. "I can always catch a quick nap later this afternoon, when the triplets do."

Maya folded her arms. "Good. That means you'll get two naps today. One this morning while I'm here, and one this afternoon."

"You might as well give up," Jesse said. "There's no talking to her when she gets stubborn."

"It's a Logan trait." Maya looked pleased rather than offended by the description.

"You get no arguments from me," her husband chimed in.

Lori still wasn't sure. "You'll wake me up if their fevers spike again?" she asked. It wasn't as if she didn't trust Maya with the triplets—the babies loved their aunt—but she wanted to be certain they hadn't developed any new symptoms.

"Of course I will. Clay and Greg can start the barn chores and I'll take care of my nieces."

"Greg? Barn chores?" Jesse looked doubtfully at his brother-in-law, dressed in wrinkle-free khaki pants and a crisp, button-down shirt.

"The pointy end of the pitchfork goes in the hay," Greg said.

"Good enough." Clay handed the spatula to his sister and clapped his brother-in-law on the shoulder. "Let's go."

"It looks like we're outnumbered." Jesse turned toward Lori, his elusive smile surfacing once again. "The p.m. shift is temporarily off-duty."

The room shrank and Maya and Clay's good-natured banter faded to a low hum in the background as their eyes met across the table.

Lori stood up so quickly the chair almost upended, and she excused herself to escape to the safety of the hallway.

Jesse had made it sound as if the two of them were a team. For a moment, she felt as if she were part of the family, instead of the woman Jesse had hired to take care of the triplets during the day.

But Lori realized she was no longer content simply to be part of a "team." What she wanted more than anything was to be part of a family. But not just *any* family.

Jesse's family.

Jesse's feet felt leaden as he stumbled back up the stairs. He decided to check on the triplets one more time, and then take Maya up on her offer to take a nap.

After he patiently gave his sister a brief recap of the triplets' sleepless night, Maya had once again taken advantage of the opportunity to remind him how blessed he was to have a nurse caring for the girls.

Not that Jesse needed to be reminded. Lori had done more than comfort the babies throughout the long night. She'd sensed how worried he was and tried to calm his fears, too.

What am I supposed to do, Lord?

This time Jesse didn't even question why it was becoming easier to turn toward God for direction, instead of away from Him.

If he were honest with himself—something that was also occurring more and more frequently—he knew Lori was partially responsible for that, too.

She hadn't backed down when he'd expressed his frustration and his doubts, but gently challenged him to look beyond his pain and return to the source of his faith. Her laughter had a way of chasing away the shadows that crowded in....

And he'd almost kissed her.

Jesse stifled a groan. Could he blame that momentary lapse of judgment on sleep deprivation? Or the fallout from being worried about the girls?

Or was it because Jesse was unable to muster up the strength to resist his feelings for Lori?

Before she moved in, he'd convinced himself that he was through with love. It had proven to be too unpredictable. Too risky.

He'd rushed into a relationship with Marie before they'd really gotten to know each other.

Jesse paused on the stairs, gripping the banister like a lifeline.

He'd tried. He'd really tried. But in the end, he'd failed to make Marie happy. Wasn't that proof he wasn't cut from the same cloth as the other men in his family? The diamond ring—the one *he'd* lost—had become a symbol over the years. A testimony of the lasting love the Logan men had found. What did it say about him, that he could keep the Circle L going but not his own marriage?

Chapter Fifteen

The wind rattled the windows, and as Lori forced her eyelids open, she became aware of two things. It was snowing. And a glance at the clock on the nightstand told her that she'd slept almost four hours.

Rolling out of bed, she immediately made her way to the nursery. All three cribs were empty. No sign of Maya and the babies. Or Jesse.

Stumbling down the stairs, she made her way to the living room, where she discovered Maya and the triplets. Brooke sat in her infant swing, happily chewing on her stuffed octopus, while Sasha and Maddie kicked contentedly on a blanket near the Christmas tree.

"Good morning," Jesse's sister greeted Lori cheerfully as she padded into the room.

"It's afternoon." Lori hadn't meant to sound so accusing.

Maya didn't take offense. "Don't blame me. I was under strict orders to let you sleep."

"Strict orders?"

Maya grinned. "Straight from the top."

Jesse. Lori's stomach did a backflip. Would he think she was shirking her duties? She had hoped he would still be asleep, too. Then he wouldn't realize she'd slept away a good portion of the day.

"How are they feeling?" Lori's gaze bounced from baby to baby, searching for signs of illness.

Maya handed Sasha a ring of chunky plastic beads. "I took their temperatures half an hour ago. Brooke and Maddie's are normal again, but Sasha's is hovering around ninety-nine."

Ninety-nine was a marked improvement. Lori couldn't hide her relief as she knelt down next to the blanket and reached for the smallest triplet. "I planned to call Dr. Cole and let her know what's going on."

"Jesse already did. The nurse said there's a twenty-four-hour bug going around, and as long as the girls are taking in fluids and their temperatures stay down, she shouldn't need to see them." Maya smiled. "She must trust they're in good hands."

Warmed by the unexpected compliment, Lori cuddled Sasha and received another reward in the form of a wide, toothless smile. "That's my girl." She glanced at Maya. "How long has Jesse been awake?"

"He staggered downstairs about two hours ago." An emotion Lori couldn't identify skimmed across the other woman's face. "We're supposed to get a few inches of snow by this evening, so he was anxious to get outside. He said he had something to do that couldn't wait."

Remembering their conversation in the garage when she'd inquired about the metal detector, Lori instantly guessed what that something was.

"He's looking for the ring."

"I think so." Maya didn't look surprised that Lori had figured out the truth. "He blames himself that it's missing."

"That's silly." Frustration bubbled up inside her. It seemed as if Jesse blamed himself for a lot of things that were beyond his control. "It wasn't as if he had any way of preventing the tornado from touching down."

Maya was silent for a moment, and her troubled expression told Lori she was reliving the events of that day. "He found the rings and the note Marie left before the tornado came through but he left them on the table, hoping Marie would change her mind."

Lori's heart sank. That explained a lot. Why Jesse felt so responsible for the missing family heirloom. And why he'd struck the word *hope* from his vocabulary. He'd added his wife's abandonment to the list of dreams that hadn't come true. Prayers he thought hadn't been answered.

Didn't he recognize all the ones that had?

"That wasn't his fault, either."

"Of course not. But my big brother, for better or worse, feels personally responsible for everything that has to do with carrying on the Logan legacy. He doesn't realize he's not the only Logan around here." Maya shook her head. "As the oldest son, he feels the weight of everyone's expectations. Considering the Circle L has been around for about a hundred and fifty years, that adds up to a lot of expectations."

Lori couldn't argue with that. Rising to her feet, she carried Sasha over to the window. Snow continued to sift from the gunmetal-gray clouds overhead, dusting the prairie grass with a layer of white.

Not far from the house, she could see the lone figure of a man on horseback, the black duster he wore a stark silhouette against the hills.

"When Clay came back to High Plains last month, I prayed that he and Jesse would move forward...but Jesse is having a difficult time letting go of the past. He can't seem to forgive our brother."

"What happened?" As soon as Lori voiced the question out loud, she wondered if Maya would think she was overstepping her bounds.

"He didn't tell you?"

Lori shook her head, hiding her surprise at Maya's assumption that Jesse had confided in her.

"It started when Clay was a teenager." Maya's eyes darkened at the memory. "He rebelled. Claimed he didn't fit in here. He questioned everything we'd been taught and it just about broke Mom and Dad's heart. One night he and some friends got into trouble. Our parents went to pick him up... The accident happened on the way home. Clay had minor injuries but Mom and Dad..."

Maya's voice hitched and Lori waited until she was able to continue with the story.

"After they died, the tension between Jesse and Clay got even worse. Clay resented it when Jesse acted like a parent instead of an older brother. The night of Clay's senior prom, right before graduation, they had a huge falling out. Jesse never told me exactly what was said, but the next morning Clay was gone. He'd packed up his things and left before Jesse went out to start his chores. Clay finally called me and we kept in touch over the years, but I couldn't convince him to come home. I prayed a lot, knowing God had the power to reach him even when I couldn't."

Lori had been praying a similar prayer for Jesse for the past few weeks. The shift in his attitude when he'd confided his doubts about his faith had proven what she'd sensed all along. Like the prairie grass after a storm, Jesse had been beaten down, but the roots of his faith hadn't been completely destroyed. If he would only take a step forward, Lori knew God would meet him on the second.

Her own life was a testimony to that.

"When Clay came back to High Plains, I thought it would mean a fresh start for them, but he told me yesterday that he's getting discouraged. He still believes Jesse has never forgiven him for the death of our parents—or for leaving the Circle L."

"Maybe it's not Clay that Jesse hasn't forgiven," Lori said softly.

"What do you mean?"

"You were just talking about how he feels responsible for everything," Lori said. "Maybe the person Jesse hasn't been able to forgive is himself."

An exercise in futility. That's what it was.

Jesse contemplated the acres of Logan land, stretching farther than the eye could see, against the chances of finding a tiny band of gold on the ground. Ground already covered with a dusting of snow.

What made him think he would find it now? He'd given up the search months ago, knowing it would be like looking for a needle in the proverbial haystack. Nothing had changed.

But I want it to.

Jesse rejected the thought. It didn't matter what he wanted. He had chosen to deal with reality. And the reality was that he still couldn't look his brother in the eye. Tomorrow was Christmas Eve and he hadn't bought gifts for anyone…and he'd fallen in love with his daughters' nanny.

How was that for reality?

Jesse closed his eyes and felt the snowflakes catch in his lashes. For a moment, he let his imagination loose. He imagined finding the ring and slipping it on Lori's finger.

A horn blasted several times and Jesse saw Maya and Greg's van rolling down the driveway.

Their departure meant Lori was awake.

He made Maya promise that she would let her sleep until she woke up on her own.

Because I'm still afraid to face her? And my feelings?

Maybe so. Or maybe, Jesse decided, he was just a glutton for punishment. So he spent another hour riding the fence line of the property where the tornado had touched down, searching for a glimmer of gold against the snow.

He finally called it quits as the sun went down. The snowflakes had changed into pellets of freezing rain that stung his face and greased the ground beneath the horse's hooves.

Jesse touched his heels against Saber's side and the horse turned agreeably toward the barn, anxious to get out of the weather, even if Jesse didn't seem to be.

He met his brother on the way out of the building.

"How are the girls?" Clay asked.

"Much better."

"I picked up the mail while I was in town." Clay handed him a stack of envelopes, most of them the size and shape of Christmas cards. "I only stopped home to feed the stock. Mayor Lawson recruited Nicki and me to help with some last-minute details at the Old Town Hall."

There was a silent question in his brother's voice that Jesse ignored. Clay and Maya would have to be content with his presence at the festivities. He couldn't offer anything more.

"I'll see you later, then." He sifted through the mail as he walked up to the house, and a red stamp caught his eye. He paused under the lamppost to read it.

Lori's name was in the top left corner, but someone had written "Return To Sender" in large block letters over the name of the addressee.

Tom Martin.

He tucked the envelopes into the inside pocket of his coat before the snow dampened them. Stepping into the inviting warmth of the house, Jesse's numb fingers fumbled with the ice-encrusted zipper on his coat.

He heard Lori's gasp before he saw her standing in the doorway. In a second she was at his side, conquering the stubborn zipper and peeling the coat off.

"I'm…"

Lori silenced him with a look and chucked his coat onto the dryer.

"Boots."

He complied immediately, sensing that if he didn't, Lori would assist him with the task. It took every ounce of his energy, but Jesse managed to scrape the frozen leather off his icy feet.

As he leaned forward, something crunched in his pocket. He'd forgotten the card.

"This is for you." He handed her the envelope he'd retrieved from his pocket. "You must have forgotten to change someone's address in your file."

Lori took it from his hand. "Thank…"

Jesse glanced at her sharply as her voice trailed off.

"Lori? What's the matter?"

She smiled wanly and tore her gaze away from the card. "I'm fine. Just a little tired. There's a fire going in the living room."

She straightened her shoulders and marched down the hall. Jesse limped along behind her.

When they reached the living room, Lori removed her knitting from the chair closest to the fire and propped her hands on her hips as Jesse gingerly lowered himself into it. Steam from a mug of coffee on the side table rose into the air, and he cast a brief but longing look at it.

"I poured it for you." Lori caught his glance.

"Is everything all right?" he asked. "You seem a little tense."

"Tense." Lori repeated the word. "Do you realize you rode off alone two hours ago? In an ice storm?"

The way Lori put it, it made him sound reckless. Irresponsible.

"You were looking for the ring, weren't you?"

And that, Jesse thought, made him sound just plain idiotic.

"I don't know why…." Except that he did. And it was her fault. Lori was beginning to make him believe that anything was possible.

"You don't understand," Jesse murmured. "The ring was entrusted to my care. Like the ranch." *Like Clay.* "You don't know what it's like to lose—" *someone* "—something that important."

"Yes, I do." The raw grief in Lori's eyes stunned him into silence. "I lost my…parents."

"I thought your mother lives in New York."

"She does." Lori's bleak smile didn't reach her eyes. "And the letter you gave to me is from my dad."

Tom Martin. Her father.

Jesse realized that he wanted her to trust him. In the past, he'd shied away from Maya's pleas to talk to her about what he was feeling, because he didn't think it would do any good. She couldn't fix it. But now he understood what his sister had really wanted. She wanted the opportunity to share his burden—something he wanted to do for Lori now.

"Will you tell me about it?"

After a split second of silence, Lori nodded.

"I told you that I'm an only child, but we were never what you would consider a close family. What I remember the most about our house was the silence. My parents didn't talk much—to each other or to me. Dad came home from work and closed himself off in the den while Mom got dinner ready. She would shoo me away whenever I tried to help. I just thought everyone's family was like ours. Until I overheard them arguing one day—about me."

A trickle of unease skated down Jesse's spine as Lori's voice ebbed away and then strengthened again.

"Mom was yelling at Dad—I'd never heard her yell before—telling him how sick she was of being blamed for ruining his life. She said things hadn't exactly turned out the way she'd planned, either." Lori paused long enough to draw a ragged breath.

"Dad said she had no right to ask him for anything, because he'd done his duty by marrying her when she got pregnant. With me. That's when it all made sense. They weren't too tired or too busy to spend time with me—

they'd never *wanted* me. I was a constant reminder that they'd buckled under the pressure from their families to do the right thing. It was hard to accept the fact I was a mistake. But even though things weren't perfect, I told myself that at least we were together. Things could always change, right?" Lori shook her head. "They did. After I graduated from high school, my parents filed for a nice, polite divorce and then they…left. It was as if they'd been freed after eighteen years of bondage. I haven't heard from Dad since."

Anger welled up inside of Jesse. It was difficult to believe that the warm, loving woman he'd come to know had grown up in such a cheerless environment. Lori could have easily become bitter or mistrustful of people.

The way I did.

Jesse winced at the thought. But instead, the trials she'd endured had forged a heart of sensitivity and compassion.

"When I started college, I was a mess," Lori continued. "It was hard to accept that my parents were out there living their own lives, but had chosen to live them without me. If it hadn't been for God bringing Lynette into my life, I don't know where I would have ended up. I didn't think I was worth loving, but she told me that God loved me. If I hadn't reached out and grabbed on to that, I think the grief would have consumed me." The warm light returned to Lori's eyes and her expression softened. "You see, I *do* understand, Jesse. There are different ways to…lose people."

Jesse didn't answer. He couldn't.

Lori was right. Didn't it feel as if he had lost his brother years ago? In some ways, the pain cut deeper than it had after Jesse lost his parents. It may have been a different kind of grief, but it was still grief.

It occurred to Jesse that Clay might be feeling the same way. Weighted down with guilt. Believing all the things Jesse had said one night out of anger.

He'd been afraid that his brother's reckless behavior would lead to another headstone next to their parents, and Jesse knew he couldn't stand by and watch it happen.

Clay thought Jesse continued to blame him for the death of their parents, but that wasn't true. Jesse blamed himself. For the death of their relationship.

Was it really possible to start over again? Rebuild?

Lori believed it was.

God can make something new. She'd told him that shortly after they met.

Now Jesse had to make a decision.

Did he believe it, too?

Chapter Sixteen

Lori retreated to her bedroom, wishing she could rewind the last twenty minutes of her life.

Flopping down on the bed, she closed her eyes—but it didn't help.

What had she been thinking? Opening up to Jesse about the wounds of her past? She didn't want his sympathy—she wanted him to know what had helped her heal those wounds.

Her cell phone hummed on the nightstand and Lori fumbled to reach it. When she saw the name that appeared on the tiny screen, she flipped it open and managed to croak out a hello.

"Lori! I'm so glad you answered the phone." Janet's brisk voice came over the line. "Do you have a minute?"

Since she planned to hide in her room as long as possible, Lori could answer the question truthfully. "Sure."

"We haven't talked for a few weeks, so I thought I'd call and find out how things are going for you."

If only Janet would have called earlier! "Things are fine." *Just peachy.* "What about you?"

"Well…" The gusty sigh accompanying the word warned Lori that she'd given her former supervisor an ideal opening. "Yvonne gave her notice yesterday and Marlene is going on maternity leave next week. I'm definitely short-staffed, and the Fraser twins are due in a few days."

"I'm sorry." Lori meant it.

"Sorry enough to come back to us?"

Janet's laughter trailed the question, but Lori wasn't fooled. And even though she'd seen this coming, it hadn't prepared her for the viselike grip around her heart.

"Janet…"

"Don't answer me right now," her supervisor interrupted. "But please hear me out."

By the time Janet was finished making an offer that she hoped Lori wouldn't refuse, Lori was more confused than ever.

Was the timing of the phone call an answer to her prayer?

Lori hung up the phone and stared at the ceiling.

What do You want me to do, Lord?

"What are you doing out here?"

Jesse started at the sound of Clay's voice. Great. Just what he needed. A witness to his total emotional breakdown.

He tried to connect his jumbled thoughts but couldn't come up with a logical reason for being out in the barn at this time of night.

Other than the real one. That it had become his refuge over the years.

"What are *you* doing here?" Jesse turned the question on his brother. "I thought you drove into High Plains to work on the Old Town Hall."

"It's almost midnight. And it's done." There was an undercurrent of pride in Clay's weary voice as he sauntered over and flopped down on a bale of hay.

Forcing Jesse to state the obvious. "If you don't mind, I'd like to be alone."

"Alone." Clay's eyebrows rose. "Are you sure that's what you want, Jess?"

Jesse scowled. "You don't want to have this conversation. Remember what happened—"

"The night I followed you into the barn." Clay finished the sentence. "How could I forget?"

Silence settled between them, the air thick with memories.

"It's in the past."

"No it isn't." Clay met his gaze. "It's right here between us. And I'm not talking about the night of the senior prom. I'm talking about the night Mom and Dad died."

No way could he take two emotional hits in the same night. Not when he was still trying to recover from the last one.

Jesse took a step forward, escape on his mind, but Clay sprang to his feet and blocked his exit.

"Remember, Jess? You caught me sneaking out and you confronted me about the decisions I'd been making. You asked me if I was sure I wanted to—and I quote— 'go down that road,' because of where it might eventually lead. I went the wrong way. I admit that and I've been paying for it ever since." Clay's voice was hoarse. "I walked away from everything I believed in, and from the woman I loved. Now I'm going to ask you the same question you asked me that night. Are you sure this is the road you want to take? Because trust me, I've been there, and it's pretty dark."

Memories crashed over Jesse, momentarily stunning him into silence. He remembered the conversation as if it had taken place yesterday.

"And Jess." Clay's voice lowered to a whisper. "You have to realize that your girls…they may follow you. Is that what you want for them?"

Hot needles stabbed the back of Jesse's eyes.

Lori had been trying to tell him the same thing when she'd opened up and shared her past. She had been raised by parents emotionally crippled because they'd been unable to forgive and move forward.

She'd been brave enough to open that door and look back at her painful past because she wanted more for the triplets. She wanted more for *him*.

Clay exhaled in frustration. "Fine. Now I know how you felt when I didn't listen to you. I always thought you were the smart one, but if you can't see what's right in front of you, then you deserve to be alone and miserable."

Jesse knew what was in front of him. The future. And for the first time in a long time, he found himself looking forward to it.

"You dump all that on me and then you leave?" Now it was Jesse's turn to step in front of his brother as he pivoted toward the door.

"You wish," Clay retorted. "When is it going to sink through your thick hide that I'm not going anywhere?"

"Now." That simple admission gave Jesse the strength to continue down a new path. His throat worked. "I'm sorry. For the things I said. For the years we lost…."

He couldn't say any more. But Jesse found that he didn't need to, because Clay reached out and gripped his hand. And gave Jesse the courage to let go of the past.

* * *

"Merry Christmas, Jesse."

Jesse's face heated as he straightened and saw Colt Ridgeway standing several feet away. Of course the chief of police had caught him lurking near the perfume counter.

"It's Christmas Eve." Jesse inched away from a display of glass bottles.

"Close enough." Colt shrugged. "Doing some last-minute shopping?"

"Really last-minute," Jesse confessed. "The triplets were sick a few days ago and I lost track of time."

Colt regarded him shrewdly. "How are you doing these days?"

"Better." Jesse smiled. "Much better."

"I'm glad to hear that, Jesse." Colt pointed to a lavender bottle on a mirrored pedestal. "By the way, Lexi likes this one. Maybe Maya would, too."

"It's not for—" Jesse caught himself, but it was too late.

A slow grin spread across the officer's face. "See you tonight."

Jesse glanced at his watch and decided to pick up the pace a little. He didn't want to buy Lori perfume—he loved the unique scent of wildflowers that she favored.

He veered down the toy aisle and picked up a net bag full of colorful tub toys. The triplets were finally starting to enjoy bath time.

So was he. Kneeling next to Lori, shoulder to shoulder with an assembly line of shampoo, bubblegum-scented bath bubbles and lotion, any worries that dogged his heels during the day dissolved.

He loved the way Lori could turn the most mundane, ordinary tasks into something extraordinary.

She said she'd lost her parents, but as far as Jesse was concerned, Tom and Roxanne Martin had lost the most when they'd pushed Lori out of their lives.

"Can't wait to get Lori Martin back on the floor…"

The familiar name snagged Jesse's attention as two women wearing warm coats over their hospital scrubs passed him.

"Janet has been stressed out since she left. I heard she called Lori yesterday and offered her a big raise if she agreed to come back to the NICU."

"I couldn't believe it when she quit to take care of the Logan triplets."

"Lori did seem to lose some of her focus after they were born. She punched out late or skipped her lunch break to spend extra time with them. I wondered if she was getting too attached to them."

Both women parted as they reached Jesse, who stood frozen in the center of the aisle.

"Well, I hope she comes to her senses. In a few years, she could be running the entire floor. It wasn't exactly a strategic career move to trade a promotion in order to work as a nanny on a ranch in the middle of nowhere…" The woman's voice faded away as she and her coworker reached the end cap and turned the corner.

It hurt to take a breath.

Lori. Leaving. And she hadn't said a word.

Don't you get it, a mocking voice chided. *This is what you get for hoping. For starting to care again.*

Fists clenched at his sides, Jesse fought against the doubts that crashed over him.

Lord, help me. I refuse to go down this path again.

As soon as Jesse prayed, it felt as if a burden were

lifted off his shoulders. His thoughts cleared as he allowed their conversation to cycle back through his mind.

It didn't sound as if Lori had agreed to return to her old job yet—only that her supervisor had asked her to come back.

It was up to him to convince her to stay. Jesse couldn't lose her now. He still hadn't told her that he and Clay reconciled. He hadn't told her how moved he'd been that she'd trusted him with the truth about her childhood.

He hadn't told her that he loved her.

Jesse closed his eyes.

Great timing, Logan. You finally come to your senses just when she's about to quit. She'll never believe you now, if you tell her that you love her.

Then he would just have to show her instead.

Galvanized into action, Jesse paid for his purchases and made his way to the parking lot. He turned the key in the ignition and felt his cell phone vibrate inside his coat pocket.

He ignored it, but less than ten seconds later it came to life again.

"Logan." He flipped open the phone and snapped out the word.

"Jesse? It's Reverend Garrison."

Jesse's heart slammed against his ribcage at the sound of the familiar voice. He knew that a call from the minister didn't necessarily mean bad news, but the conversation he'd overheard in the store had put him on edge.

"What can I do for you?"

"I was wondering if you could stop by the church for a few minutes. We need to…talk."

Jesse frowned. A minister who needed to talk. Something in the man's voice warned him that the conversation wasn't going to center around the weather.

What he wanted to do was get home to Lori. To tell her that he was in love with her. To beg her not to leave.

"It won't take long."

Five minutes would be too long. Especially when he'd been so resistant to the truth of his feelings for Lori. "I don't think I—"

"Please, Jesse."

Jesse sighed. Even though he'd resisted Reverend Garrison's attempts to draw him back into the fold after Marie died, the man had patiently waited in the wings, praying for him until Jesse came to his senses. The way a lot of other people had.

Which meant Jesse owed him a few minutes of his time.

"I'm on my way."

"Thanks. We'll be in my office."

We'll?

Jesse was about to ask who else would be there, but the minister hung up before he could question him.

Main Street was a flurry of activity. Most of the stores were closing early, so last-minute Christmas shoppers trudged through the snow, laden down with packages. Jesse noticed with amusement that most of them were men. He passed the Garrison building where Maya worked, and saw customers lined up outside of Elmira's Pie Diner, waiting for their orders.

The church parking lot was jam-packed with cars, but Jesse managed to maneuver his pickup into one of the few empty spaces.

He still couldn't believe the volunteers had finished rebuilding the Old Town Hall in time for the Christmas Eve celebration.

Mayor Lawson had invited him to speak at the Founders' Day potluck that evening, but Jesse had turned down the invitation. As far as he'd been concerned, he was the last person qualified to give a speech on "Moving Forward in Faith."

Now? Jesse smiled as he remembered his conversation with Clay. Now he just might have something to say.

Reverend Garrison stepped out of his office and waved to Jesse a split second after the front doors of the church closed behind him.

Jesse was used to seeing an easy smile on Michael's face, but today deep lines bracketed his mouth and his expression looked too serious for a simple social call.

Michael stepped to one side as Jesse warily approached. "I appreciate this, Jesse. Come in."

Jesse stepped into the office but stopped short as Heather Waters rose to her feet. He gave the attractive young woman a polite nod, a little mystified by her presence. Heather had returned to High Plains after a ten-year absence to assist the victims of the tornado, but because she was closer in age to his sister, Maya, he didn't remember much about her.

"Hello, Jesse." Heather's smile, like Reverend Garrison's, appeared forced.

The minister closed the door, effectively sealing them all inside the office. "You've met Avery. My niece."

For the first time, Jesse noticed the teenage girl huddled in one of the comfortable leather chairs, hugging her knees against her chest. Two brown pigtails didn't conceal her pale features as she stared intently at her lap.

"Of course. She helped Tommy and Layla decorate my Christmas tree one afternoon."

Avery mumbled something but didn't look up.

"Have a seat, Jesse." Reverend Garrison motioned to an empty chair.

Jesse hesitated. He didn't want a seat. Not when Lori could be packing her suitcase.

"Please."

Another *please*.

Jesse buried a sigh and sat down. "What's this about?" His impatience to get back to the Circle L—and to Lori—honed an edge on the words.

"Avery has something to tell you," Heather said softly.

The girl glanced at him and then quickly looked away, but not before Jesse saw a flare of panic in her eyes.

"Okay." Whatever was going on, Jesse didn't want to be responsible for making a kid like Avery shake in her boots. He stretched out his legs as if he had all the time in the world, and aimed a smile in her direction.

His plan backfired. Instead of putting her at ease, Avery slumped even lower in the chair and shot a distressed look at her uncle. Compassion filled Reverend Garrison's eyes, but he simply nodded.

"I wanted…" Avery choked on the words as she met Jesse's gaze. "I wanted to tell you that I'm the one who put the fake ring in the Lost and Found a few months ago."

"You?" Jesse frowned.

Avery nodded miserably, tears springing to her eyes. "It looked kind of like the one everyone was searching for, but I didn't know for sure. I figured whoever lost it could buy a new one, and I wanted to keep the one I found. But then Uncle Mike said it was really old and it meant a lot to the person who lost it. That it was special. I never owned anything like that before but when I came to your house that night with Maya, I could tell that you were sad it was gone. I'm really sorry. I know I messed up."

Her voice trailed off and Reverend Garrison put a comforting hand on the girl's shoulder while Jesse tried to fit the pieces together.

Wait a second. Several of the words connected, and a cautious hope stirred in Jesse's chest.

"Are you saying…" His throat tightened. "That you *found* the diamond ring? The real one?"

Avery sniffed. And nodded. Before Jesse realized what was happening, she opened her hand. Cradled in her palm was the diamond ring that Will Logan had slipped on Emmeline's finger when he'd proposed.

Jesse stared at it in disbelief.

"Avery showed the ring to me this morning and I recognized it right away." Reverend Garrison's voice was apologetic. "We talked it over and decided you should be the one to determine the punishment."

"Punishment?" Jesse found his voice and grinned, startling the three people in the room. "Are you kidding? Avery deserves a reward."

He couldn't believe it had turned up after all this time. Today. This was no coincidence. This was an answer to prayer that took his breath away. A tangible symbol of God's continued faithfulness.

"Reward…" Reverend Garrison repeated the word cautiously. "I don't think you understand, Jesse. Avery found the diamond and *kept* it. She knows she should have come forward sooner—"

"I think Avery came forward at *exactly* the right time," Jesse interrupted. His hand shook as he took the ring from Avery. "I was going to replace it. Today, as a matter of fact."

Heather gasped and understanding dawned in Reverend Garrison's eyes.

"You…" Avery's eyes filled with tears. "You aren't going to call the police?"

"Everyone deserves a second chance." Jesse's hand shook as he slipped the ring into his shirt pocket. "Now if you'll excuse me, I'm going to ask for mine."

Chapter Seventeen

Lori placed Maddie's stocking on one of the weighted gold hooks on the mantel and stepped back to critique her effort.

All three stockings hung over the fireplace now—each one as unique as the precious baby she had made it for. As a last-minute change to the original design, Lori had trimmed the top of each stocking with a row of tiny jingle bells.

She had stayed up until her eyes began to cross, in order to finish the stockings in time for the gift opening that would take place at Maya and Greg's house on Christmas Day.

After the triplets were in their cribs for the night, she planned to finish wrapping the stocking stuffers she'd bought, while Jesse attended the potluck at the newly finished Old Town Hall.

For a moment, Lori let her imagination form a picture of the two of them attending the celebration together.

She shook the thought away. Why continue to torture herself?

Help me be content with what I have, Lord, and not want more.

After Janet's phone call, Lori had been awake most of the night, asking God to give her the wisdom to make the right decision. Given her conflicted emotions, the temptation to return to a stable job—one in which she didn't have to interact with Jesse on a daily basis—was overwhelming.

Her supervisor had practically begged her to return to the hospital, and Lori wondered if Janet's offer was divine intervention. Was God providing a way out?

But as the night wore on and she continued to pray about the matter, she had come to a conclusion.

She wouldn't leave. As long as Jesse needed her, she would stay at the Circle L. No matter the risk to her own heart, she was committed. She loved the triplets.

And she loved Jesse.

Lori had come to that conclusion during the wee hours of the morning, too.

She knew that part of Jesse's resistance, when it came to trusting people, stemmed from being abandoned. Lori refused to be one of the people he could add to his list of those who'd left. Like it or not, he was stuck with her.

The doorbell chimed and Lori paused to straighten the sofa cushions on her way to answer it. She wasn't expecting company, but since it was Christmas Eve, it was possible the postal service was making last-minute deliveries.

"Hello!" On the other side of the door stood a young woman in her early twenties.

"Can I help you?"

"I'm Melissa Olson." She gave Lori a wide smile. "And I'm here to help you."

Lori looked at her in confusion. "I don't understand."

"I'm here to babysit the triplets."

"I think there's been some kind of mistake." There had to be some kind of mistake! "Are you sure you have the right address?"

Melissa stomped her feet, depositing the snow that clung to her fashionable half boots onto the welcome mat in front of the door. "This is the Circle L, right?"

"Yes."

"Then I'm at the right address." She must have sensed Lori's indecision. "Mr. Logan called me," she added, as if that tidbit of information might be the key to getting past Lori and into the warm house.

Jesse had hired her? On Christmas Eve?

Lori bit her lip. Jesse had been gone since breakfast, and although he'd left a brief note explaining that he had some shopping to do, she couldn't help but wonder if the passionate retelling of her less-than-perfect childhood the night before had something to do with his disappearance.

It was entirely possible that she was looking at her replacement!

Melissa shivered. "Um, it's kind of cold out here...."

"I'm sorry. Please, come in," Lori said automatically.

The girl looked relieved as she entered the house, shedding her coat, scarf and mittens on the way in.

"Did ah, Mr. Logan...mention how long you would be watching the triplets?"

"No. He just said he'd pay me double. Poor college students like myself don't ask a lot of questions."

Well, Lori had a lot of questions. The most important one was why Jesse had hired a sitter for the babies, when she'd planned to stay with them that evening.

"But—"

"Don't worry about a thing," Melissa interrupted breezily. "I'm the oldest of six, and two of my brothers are twins. The babies are in good hands."

"I'm sure they are," Lori said weakly. "But I don't have plans to…go anywhere tonight."

"Really? Because Mr. Logan said you should be ready to leave at five-thirty."

"Ready to leave?" Lori squeaked.

"Yup. That's what he said. He'll be waiting out front." Melissa looked around the room. "Where are the babies? I can't wait to play with them."

"They should be waking up soon." Lori pulled the baby monitor out of her sweater pocket.

Melissa plucked it out of her hand. "Don't you want to change? You've only got fifteen minutes." A pair of wide green eyes looked pointedly at her long-sleeve T-shirt and comfortable jeans.

Lori grimaced. "I suppose I should."

She ran upstairs, opened up the closet and grabbed the green velvet dress she'd worn to the hospital Christmas party the year before. With its full skirt and sequined bodice, it was probably a little fancy for a church potluck, but she didn't exactly have a lot of time to choose an alternative.

A few minutes later, a soft tap on the door interrupted her thoughts. Melissa's lilting voice penetrated the wood. "It's five-thirty!"

"I'll be right down." Lori's hands shook as she twisted her hair into a casual knot at the base of her neck, securing it with a pearl clip. She stepped into a pair of black ballet flats and flew down the stairs.

A quick peek into the living room told her that Melissa seemed to have everything under control. All three babies were awake and appeared to be fascinated by the new face in the room.

Lori went around and kissed each baby, resisting the urge to give the sitter detailed instructions. Melissa looked quite capable, and she had already coaxed a gurgle of laughter out of Sasha.

Grabbing her wool coat from the hall closet, Lori slipped out the door.

"Merry Christmas!"

Clay stood by the car, waiting for her. Lori managed a smile even as her heart sank.

Mr. Logan.

Of course. Clay was the one who'd arranged for a babysitter, most likely at Nicki's request. Clay's fiancée had expressed her disappointment that Lori wouldn't be joining them for the Christmas Eve festivities. Nicki and Clay had been hard at work on the Old Town Hall and had obviously put their heads together to come up with a plan to include her after all.

Clay opened the door on the passenger side and Lori slid inside the vehicle. She was tempted to ask where Jesse was but half-afraid of what Clay's answer would be.

How would he react when he found out that Clay and Nicki had hired another babysitter for his daughters?

On the way to High Plains, Clay entertained her with humorous stories about the work crew's latest bloopers while they scrambled to finish the last-minute details in time.

By the time they arrived at the gathering, the snow-covered churchyard was already filled with members of the congregation and visitors from the community.

A large section of the park—from the restored gazebo

to the Old Town Hall—had been decorated for the occasion. Tea lights flickered inside the luminaries that lined the sidewalk leading up to the church, and evergreen swags were wound around the old-fashioned lampposts. Instrumental Christmas music played softly in the background, a perfect accompaniment to the laughter and conversation.

Clay, who'd been more than anxious to reach his fiancée's side, strode ahead of Lori while she paused to absorb the peaceful beauty of the surroundings. By the time she located him again, he stood at Nicki's side, Kasey perched on his broad shoulders.

The rest of Jesse's family clustered nearby, talking with Reverend Garrison and Heather, whose arm was linked with Avery's.

Lori smiled as she saw Tommy, a miniature replica of Greg in a navy suit and red bow tie, hunkered on the ground between his parents, surreptitiously building a tiny snowman.

But where was Jesse? And why didn't it seem to trouble his family that he wasn't there to share in the celebration?

Layla spotted Lori, and with a cry of delight broke away from the group.

"Lori! Lori!" The little girl ran up to her, the skirt of her wintergreen taffeta dress belling out above tiny, fur-trimmed boots. "I have a pretty dress, too. And sparkles on my mittens. See?"

"Your dress is very pretty," Lori agreed. "And I wish I had sparkles on my mittens."

Layla beamed.

"Were you surprised?" Maya joined them, stunning in

a crimson wool suit and matching hat. She reeled Lori in
for a brief hug and lowered her voice to a whisper. "I
know it's hard for you to leave my nieces for a few hours,
but you need a break occasionally, too!"

Lori was surprised and touched by Maya's warm
greeting. How was it that in such a short time, she'd fallen
in love with Jesse's entire family? Maybe it wouldn't
hurt for one night—tonight—to pretend she really
belonged with this precious group of people. It would be
a Christmas gift to herself.

"It was nice of you to arrange for a sitter."

Maya's brown eyes danced with sudden mischief. "Oh,
don't thank me."

Lori nodded in understanding. Nicki must have engi-
neered the surprise, just as she'd suspected.

"Did Clay tell you that we have something else to celebrate tonight?" Maya glanced over her shoulder. "Greg
and I signed Tommy's final adoption papers this morning."

Now Lori hugged her. "That's wonderful, Maya."

"Tommy said that now we are, and I quote, 'a forever
family.' And then he wondered why we were crying!"

A forever family. Lori felt the familiar ache inside, even
though she rejoiced with the couple over the good news.
An image of Jesse and the triplets flashed in her mind.

Help me be content with the way things are, Lord.

"There's a larger turnout than we anticipated." Greg
walked over and tucked Maya against his side. "Michael
wants to gather around the tree out here, and sing some
Christmas hymns before the service begins."

Lori summoned a smile as the minister approached.
She'd prayed Jesse would have a change of heart and
attend the service. She wasn't sure if she could enjoy the

evening, knowing that he had, once again, distanced himself from the people who loved him.

Scraping up her courage, she decided to ask if anyone knew where he was. It wasn't like Jesse to abandon his chores and disappear for an entire day. "Maya, do you know—"

"Look, Mommy! There's a horse!" A childish voice suddenly broke through the quiet hum of conversation and the crowd's attention shifted to the street.

"It's a sleigh," someone murmured.

People craned their necks to get a better look. Kasey, still perched on Clay's shoulders, pointed a chubby finger and giggled.

"Maybe it's Santa," Layla said, wide-eyed.

Tommy's nose wrinkled. "That's not Santa. It's Uncle Jesse."

Lori's heart gave a little kick. It couldn't be. Jesse Logan and the musical jingle of bells did *not* go together.

Several people shifted, and she caught a glimpse of the sleigh as it came to a gliding stop next to the curb. A familiar figure dropped the reins and stood up, scanning the crowd.

Heads began to turn as curious faces looked to Reverend Michael for an explanation.

"Don't look at me." The young minister shrugged, but there was a knowing sparkle in his eyes. "This isn't part of the program."

"Lori?"

She froze when Jesse called out her name.

Clay grinned and gave her a friendly nudge. "I think that's you."

"But…" Panic choked off Lori's ability to finish the sentence.

"Go on." Maya gave her hand a reassuring squeeze. "I think my big brother has something to say to you."

"Finally," Clay muttered under his breath.

On their own accord, Lori's feet carried her forward. She felt people's smiles as they moved aside to let her pass.

Within moments she reached the sleigh.

And Jesse.

Chapter Eighteen

Jesse took a deep breath as Lori looked up at him, a confused expression on her lovely face.

God, I know You've been more than generous but I could use a little more help right about now.

Panicked, he tried to remember the speech he'd rehearsed on his way into town. If he said too much—or not enough—he could lose Lori forever. And now here they were, surrounded by dozens of curious faces who had pushed even closer to see what was going on.

Lori reached out to stroke Saber's nose. The gelding's appreciative snort came out in a plume of frost. "Is this part of the celebration? Horse-drawn carriage rides?"

Jesse blinked. Was it possible that Lori still didn't know what she meant to him? Why he was here?

How do I convince her, Lord?

With a flash of insight, he understood. In spite of Lori's strong faith, she still bore the scars of her childhood. The painful memory of parents who had never valued—or loved—her for the remarkable, beautiful person she was.

It was up to him to tell her.

Jesse knew what he had to do, even though his mouth went dry as dust at the thought. He had hoped everyone would be inside the Old Town Hall by the time he arrived. His original plan had been to wait for Lori to come out after the service so he could coax her into going for a sleigh ride with him. Once they were on their way, he would find a quiet, secluded place by the river to tell her how he felt about her.

Now he saw God's hand at work and he knew what would convince her that his feelings were real.

"I'm not giving sleigh rides," Jesse said. "I'm..." He was trying to propose, but he couldn't say that out loud or it would ruin the proposal. "I'm making a memory. For the girls. Like you suggested."

Great. He sounded as stilted and awkward as a kindergartner learning to read, but given the circumstances, short, choppy sentences were the best he could do. Especially when Lori was absolutely take-a-man's-breath-away beautiful. The sequins on her dress sparkled in the lamplight and the soft fabric traced the curves of her slender frame.

In spite of the chilly temperatures, Jesse broke out in a sweat.

Lori gave him a quizzical smile. "But the girls aren't here."

Jesse forgot about the crowd. He had Lori's attention and he wasn't going to lose it. He wasn't going to lose *her*.

He jumped down from the sleigh and went down on one knee in the snow. A murmur rippled through the people watching and Lori gasped when Jesse took her hand.

"This will be something the girls can tell their children someday. And their children's children."

Lori's hand fluttered in his but she didn't pull it away, which gave him the courage to go on. "I love you, Lori. You came into my life and you…you changed it. You changed me. Because of you, I found my faith again. We haven't known each other very long, but I know that I want to laugh with you and cry with you and grow old with you. I wish I could tell you how much you mean to me, but I've never been good with words…."

And he ran out of them. Just like that. But maybe words weren't that important, Jesse decided. Because the expression on Lori's face told him everything he needed to know.

"Jesse Logan," Lori whispered his name. "You're better at finding the words than you think you are. It's one of the reasons I fell in love with you."

Jesse felt as if his heart was going to pound its way out of his chest. He pulled a small velvet box from his coat pocket.

Then he gave her a lopsided smile. "I was hoping you'd say that."

Lori's eyes widened. "What is that?"

"Part of the memory." He opened the cover and Emmeline's diamond winked up at them.

"You found the ring." Lori stared at the antique ring in awe. "What an incredible…gift."

Jesse had to disagree. He might have thought so before he'd met Lori, but now he realized that love was the true cornerstone of the Logan family legacy. Not the Circle L. Not the diamond ring.

That's what he had to convince Lori to believe.

"I found *you,* Lori. As far as I'm concerned, your love is the gift. Will you be my wife?"

She clapped her hand over her lips and nodded wordlessly.

Jesse slipped the ring on her finger. Out of the corner of his eye, he saw Maya and Nicki clinging to each other. Greg had perched Tommy on his shoulders for a better view while Layla bounced up and down and clapped her hands.

Jesse smiled and rose to his feet. "I think the entire community is going to be part of our memory."

Lori smiled back as he drew her into his arms. Her breath stirred his hair as she whispered in his ear.

"I wouldn't have it any other way."

Jesse closed his eyes. Neither would he. And he thought of another way to show her that he meant it.

He kissed her. In front of everyone.

Dazed, Lori opened her eyes when Jesse reluctantly released her. All around them, people were clapping and whistling.

Reverend Garrison stood a few feet away, a wide smile on his face.

"This wasn't exactly what I had in mind when I asked Jesse Logan if he would say a few words at the dedication of the Old Town Hall this evening."

Laughter rippled through the crowd and Lori felt the color flood into her cheeks. Jesse winked at her, his fingers tightening around hers. She couldn't help but glance down at the diamond on her finger, still caught in the afterglow of Jesse's proposal.

He *loved* her. He claimed that he wasn't good with words, and yet he'd proposed to her in front of his friends and family. In front of the entire town.

God, You are so good. Thank You for bringing us together.

Michael cleared his throat. "That said, in all honesty,

I can't think of a better way to start this service—on the eve of our Savior's birth—than with an expression of love like the one Jesse just showed us," he said. "The ring he placed on Lori Martin's finger is the same ring that Will Logan gave to his intended bride—a pledge of his love and his commitment before God, to stay by her side no matter what the future held. The past few months have been difficult for our community, but we're here together, standing in the very same place the first settlers gathered years ago. Not only to celebrate the completion of the Old Town Hall but to celebrate God's faithfulness. He has not—nor will He ever—abandon His people."

A chorus of *amens* burst out and tears banked behind Lori's eyes.

"People lost many things in the tornado, but the one thing we didn't lose was hope. Hope in God and faith in one another. It was those two things that moved Will Logan and Zeb Garrison to put a stake near the river on Christmas Day in 1858 and claim the empty sea of prairie grass around it. They named that place High Plains. According to local history, those men fell in love with two remarkable women—Emmeline Carter and Nora Mitchell." Michael paused and a smile teased the corners of his lips. "Although, from what I've read in the town archives, those relationships were not without challenges and trials. God was at work in their lives, too, and love prevailed." For a moment, Michael's gaze lingered on Heather Waters and a look of understanding passed between them.

Lori saw Clay and Nicki also exchange a tender glance. She knew they weren't the only couple who could relate to the truth of the minister's words. Many of the couples she saw had allowed God to work in their lives after the storm.

Her gaze moved from Jesse's brother and his fiancée to Nicki's close friend, Josie Cane, who stood in the protective circle of Silas Marstow's arms. Their daughters, Alyssa and Lily, stood beside them, hands clasped.

Not far away, Colt Ridgeway and Lexi Harmon had eyes only for each other.

"To dedicate the rebuilding of the Old Town Hall tonight, I would like to share a verse with you. My heartfelt prayer is that it will remind everyone of God's amazing love for us. I found this written inside the cover of the pulpit bible that Will Logan donated to High Plains Community Church after a tornado struck the town in 1860. The words are as true for us today as they were for the people that Will wanted to encourage back then."

"Yet this I call to mind and therefore I have hope. Because of the Lord's great love we are not consumed, for His compassions never fail. They are new every morning."

Lori felt the jolt that coursed through Jesse, as Michael quietly recited the same verse she had shared with him the night the girls had been sick. The one that had encouraged her to believe and trust God's love.

Michael bowed his head. "Please join me in a word of prayer."

Lori closed her eyes and the tears leaked out. She felt Jesse's fingertips gently brush them away.

"Lord God—" Michael stopped as a dog began to bark nearby. He would have continued, but Tommy's sudden shout echoed around the churchyard.

"It's Charlie!"

"Tommy, no." Greg choked out as the little boy broke away from the group. "It can't be him."

Tommy kept going. At the sound of the boy's voice, the dog turned and limped out of the shadows, tail wagging.

Everyone watched, awestruck, as Tommy dropped to his knees. Charlie barreled into his arms and the two wrestled together in the snow.

"It *is* Charlie." Maya clapped a hand over her mouth.

"Tommy *said* that Charlie would be home for Christmas." Layla looked at the adults around her, perplexed by their reaction. "Didn't you believe him?"

"The faith of a child," Reverend Garrison murmured.

"Home for Christmas," Jesse repeated softly. "What do you think?"

Lori tilted her head. "I like the sound of that."

"You're my home, Lori," he murmured. "You and the girls."

Her lips curved into a smile. "I like the sound of that even more."

Reverend Garrison shook his head, his expression bemused by the unexpected interruption. "We've witnessed God at work tonight in amazing ways. As we sit down to eat together, I encourage everyone to share some of the things that God has done in your lives over the past few months."

Jesse smiled down at Lori. "Should I go first?"

Lori rested her cheek against his shoulder, her heart full. "Maybe *I* should."

Jesse glanced at his brother and Clay gave them a knowing wink. "I think all of us will have something to say. It might take a while."

And it did. People gathered around the tables and the celebrations continued well into the evening, as dozens of stories were told of God's faithfulness. After the storm.

* * * * *

Want more High Plains?
Don't miss Will and Emmeline's story in
HIGH PLAINS BRIDE by Valerie Hansen,
the first book in the heartwarming new
AFTER THE STORM: THE FOUNDING YEARS *series*
available in January 2010
from Love Inspired Historical.

Dear Reader,

Like Jesse Logan, sometimes we encounter "storms" in our lives. The aftermath can leave us feeling shattered or confused, wondering if God has abandoned us.

If you are experiencing, or have recently encountered, one of life's storms, I pray you will be encouraged by the verse from Lamentations that Lori Martin shared with Jesse. Our hope does indeed come from the Lord. Because of His great love, we are not consumed—His compassions are new *every* morning.

God is not only a firm foundation but He rebuilds damaged hearts and lives—that is a promise you can believe.

Wishing you peace and joy this Christmas season!

Kathryn Springer

QUESTIONS FOR DISCUSSION

1. What was Lori's first impression of Jesse Logan? Was it accurate? Why did she offer to take care of the triplets? In what way did her background influence her decision?

2. What was Jesse's first impression of Lori? Why did he assume Lori had never gone through pain or disappointment?

3. Describe a time or event in your life when you discovered the truth of the verse in Philippians (4:13) that says, "I can do all things through Christ who gives me strength?"

4. What aspects of Jesse's character does Lori come to admire?

5. What did the heirloom engagement ring symbolize to Jesse? Why did losing it impact him so greatly?

6. Why did Jesse keep people, including his own brother, at arm's length?

7. Jesse and Clay's estrangement was rooted in miscommunication and misunderstanding. Have you ever experienced a similar situation? What was the outcome?

8. Why was celebrating Christmas so important to Lori? What are some special family traditions that you continue in your own family?

9. How did the losses that Jesse experienced shape his perspective? In what ways did Lori help him find hope again?

10. What was the turning point in Jesse and Lori's relationship?

11. How did forgiveness play a significant role in both of their lives? Why is it sometimes easier to forgive others than it is to forgive ourselves?

12. What was your favorite scene in the book? Why?

13. Why do you think that Jesse chose to propose to Lori the way he did? What "prop" was significant and why?

14. Why was it significant that Jesse asked his brother and sister for help on Christmas Eve? How did it reflect his heart change?

15. How is the theme of "rebuilding" lived out in the characters' lives? Emotionally and spiritually? Have you ever had to "rebuild" something in your own life? Why? What was it?

Here is an exciting sneak preview of
TWIN TARGETS by Marta Perry,
the first book in the new 6-book
Love Inspired Suspense series
PROTECTING THE WITNESSES
available beginning January 2010.

Deputy U.S. Marshal Micah McGraw forced down the sick feeling in his gut. A law enforcement professional couldn't get emotional about crime victims. He could imagine his police chief father saying the words. Or his FBI agent big brother. They wouldn't let emotion interfere with doing the job.

"Pity." The local police chief grunted.

Natural enough. The chief hadn't known Ruby Maxwell, aka Ruby Summers. He hadn't been the agent charged with relocating her to this supposedly safe environment in a small village in Montana. He didn't have to feel responsible for her death.

"This looks like a professional hit," Chief Burrows said.

"Yeah."

He knew only too well what was in the man's mind. What would a professional hit man be doing in the remote reaches of western Montana? Why would anyone want to kill this seemingly inoffensive waitress?

And most of all, what did the U.S. Marshals Service have to do with it?

All good questions. Unfortunately he couldn't answer

any of them. Secrecy was the crucial element that made the Federal Witness Protection Service so successful. Breach that, and everything that had been gained in the battle against organized crime would be lost.

His cell buzzed and he turned away to answer it. "McGraw."

"You wanted the address for the woman's next of kin?" asked one of his investigators.

"Right." Ruby had a twin sister, he knew. She'd have to be notified. Since she lived back east, at least he wouldn't be the one to do that.

"Jade Summers. Librarian. Current address is 45 Rock Lane, White Rock, Montana."

For an instant Micah froze. "Are you sure of that?"

"'Course I'm sure."

After he hung up, Micah turned to stare once more at the empty shell that had been Ruby Summers. She'd made mistakes in her life, plenty of them, but she'd done the right thing in the end when she'd testified against the mob. She hadn't deserved to end up lifeless on a cold concrete floor.

As for her sister…

What exactly was an easterner like Jade Summers doing in a small town in Montana? If there was an innocent reason, he couldn't think of it.

Ruby must have tipped her off to her location. That was the only explanation, and the deed violated one of the major principles of witness protection.

Ruby had known the rules. Immediate family could be relocated with her. If they chose not to, no contact was permitted—ever.

Ruby's twin had moved to Montana. White Rock was

probably forty miles or so east of Billings. Not exactly around the corner from her sister.

But the fact that she was in Montana had to mean that they'd been in contact. And that contact just might have led to Ruby's death.

He glanced at his watch. Once his team arrived, he'd get back on the road toward Billings and beyond, to White Rock. To find Jade Summers and get some answers.

* * * * *

*Will Micah get to Jade in time to save
her from a similar fate?
Find out in TWIN TARGETS,
available January 2010
from Love Inspired Suspense.*

The wagon train was supposed to lead the Carter family to a fresh start. But when a tornado tears their family apart and strands the survivors in High Plains, Kansas, Emmeline Carter needs all the help town founder Will Logan can give to hold her family together.

Here is a sneak peek of HIGH PLAINS BRIDE by Valerie Hansen, Book 1 in the AFTER THE STORM: THE FOUNDING YEARS series available January 2010 from Love Inspired® Historical.

AFTER
the **STORM**
The Founding Years

* * *

AT FIRST, Emmeline feared that the distant Indians had decided to approach. Then, she realized that the horseman was riding with saddle and bridle as well as wearing a slicker that flapped out behind him like great, black wings. No Indian would ride or dress like that, at least not any she had seen thus far in her travels.

She held up her arms, waved boldly and shouted to the rider. "Over here. Hurry! We need help."

He slid off his mount and started to run toward her before the horse had come to a complete stop.

She knew that man. Glory be! It was the cowboy from the mercantile. And no one had ever looked better to her, not even erstwhile beaux from her old home town.

Unable to recall his name, she nevertheless greeted him with unbounded enthusiasm. Clasping her hands she shouted, "Hallelujah!"

"What's happened? Are you all right?"

"Some of us are," Emmeline answered, sobering and glancing over her shoulder toward the place where the remains of the ox still lay. "The important thing right now is rescuing my mother. She's trapped under the wagon. My brother and I tried to lift it but it was too heavy."

Will was fetching his rope from where it was tied at the fork of his saddle. "Where's your father? We'll need all the muscle we can get."

Emmeline lowered her voice. "Papa will not be helping. He's gone to meet his Maker."

The cowboy merely nodded and went to work instead of asking for further explanation.

Relieved, Emmeline sighed. There was really nothing else to say. When the last breath had left her father's body, their whole life had changed. They had no home, no money to speak of, very few possessions and no predictable future. She didn't know how things could get any worse.

And then she remembered that Bess and the twins were still missing.

* * *

Can Will, and the town of High Plains, help the Carters heal?
Find out in HIGH PLAINS BRIDE available in January 2010
only from Love Inspired® Historical.

TITLES AVAILABLE NEXT MONTH

Available December 29, 2009

FINDING HER WAY HOME by Linda Goodnight
Redemption River

She came to Oklahoma to escape her past, but single dad Trace Bowman isn't about to let Cheyenne Rhodes hide her heart away. But will he stand by her when he learns the secret she's running from?

THE DOCTOR'S PERFECT MATCH by Irene Hannon
Lighthouse Lane

Dr. Christopher Morgan is *not* looking for love. Especially with Marci Clay. The physician and the waitress come from two very different worlds. Worlds that are about to collide in faith and love.

HER FOREVER COWBOY by Debra Clopton
Men of Mule Hollow

Mule Hollow, Texas, is chock-full of handsome cowboys. Veterinarian Susan Worth moves in, dreaming of meeting Mr. Right, who most certainly is *not* the gorgeous rescue worker blazing through town...or *is* he?

THE FAMILY NEXT DOOR by Barbara McMahon

Widower Joe Kincaid doesn't want his daughter liking their pretty new neighbor. His little girl's lost too much already. And he doesn't think the city girl will last a month in their small Maine town. But Gillian Parker isn't what he expected.

A SOLDIER'S DEVOTION by Cheryl Wyatt
Wings of Refuge

Pararescue jumper Vince Reardon doesn't want to accept Valentina Russo's heartfelt apologies for wrecking his motorcycle.... Until she shows this soldier what true devotion is really about.

MENDING FENCES by Jenna Mindel

Called home to care for her ailing mother, Laura Toivo finds herself in uncertain territory. With the help of neighbor Jack Stahl, she'll learn that life is all about connections, and that love is the greatest gift.

LICNMBPA1209